'Lynn Doyle' was the pen name [...] (1873–1961), a bank manager fro[...] his first story while working as a cl[...] the Northern Banking Company.

His pseudonym is typical of his sense of fun – early in his writing career, he happened to notice a can marked *Linseed Oil* in a grocer's shop, and so 'Lynn C. Doyle' was born. Later he dropped the 'C.' (he may have felt it was too 'literary') and settled on the name familiar to generations of Irish readers.

AN ULSTER CHILDHOOD

BY LYNN DOYLE

Author of " Ballygullion," etc.

THE
BLACKSTAFF
PRESS
BELFAST AND DOVER, NEW HAMPSHIRE

First published in 1921
by Maunsel and Roberts Ltd
This Blackstaff Press edition is a photolithographic
facsimile of the second edition published by Duckworth
and printed by The Burleigh Press, 1926.

This edition published in 1985
by The Blackstaff Press
3 Galway Park, Dundonald, Belfast BT16 0AN, Northern Ireland
and
51 Washington Street, Dover, New Hampshire 03820 USA
with the assistance of
The Arts Council of Northern Ireland

Printed in Northern Ireland
by The Universities Press Limited

British Library Cataloguing in Publication Data

Doyle, Lynn
An Ulster childhood
I. Title
823'.912[F]   PR6025.044
ISBN 0 85640 349 0

PREFACE

THIS little book is not an autobiography. Neither the characters nor the incidents are taken unaltered from life. Not even the little boy is true, though the author set out to tell the truth about him. But a " grown-up " cannot tell the truth about a little boy, even if he would. In spite of himself humour and sadness will creep in ; and little boys have not enough experience of life to be either humorous or sad. So it is the grown-up author who has written the book, and not the little boy he used to be. But the author does not feel that the public is thereby wholly cheated, remembering how often in the writing of it he became that little boy again.

CONTENTS

THE LENAGHANS

SOME time ago, rummaging in a box of family papers, I came on an old wages book of a farm in the County Down. There were no dates given, but I surmise that it went back to about fifty years ago. One of the entries ran, " J. Lenaghan, half a year's wages as second ploughman, £4 10s." The entry set me thinking; for I remembered J. Lenaghan. Those were the days when a ploughman sometimes remained with one master his whole lifetime, and J. Lenaghan flourished as late as my boyhood. Perhaps " flourished " is not the word; it would be more accurate to say " existed." I recall J. Lenaghan very clearly, a tall, stooped man, with a shock of black hair turning a little grey, and a sallow, melancholy visage. It was no wonder if he was melancholy. He cannot have had much cause for mirth. He married late in life for an agricultural labourer, and of his six or seven living children—I cannot remember the exact number— none was old enough to help him. Prices were then much cheaper than they are in these days of war; yet at the very best, when one divides nine pounds a year by a woman and six children the quotient is small. It is hard to see how the thing could be done.

Yet it was done, though with sad pinching and distress. I have heard the little Lenaghans crying many a time as I went past the house at bed-time, and I used to blame their mother for being a cross woman, and feared and avoided her ; but I think now that I wronged her, and that hungry little stomachs and little cold chilblained feet were the cause of most of the wailing ; and when I remember her pale, patient face I am sorry for my childish sitting in judgment.

But in those days it never entered my head, nor the heads of people a great deal older and wiser than I, that the Lenaghans were being hardly dealt with at all. We spoke rather more about the will of Providence than we do now, though perhaps we practised it less, and we thought it was the will of Providence that a ploughman should be paid only nine pounds a year, and that his wife and children should always be hungry, and himself and they scarcely enough clad for decency, let alone warmth and comeliness. We thought that Providence sent such folk on earth poor and kept them so, that we might pity them a little when we had time to spare from our eating and drinking and amusement to remember their sad case, and give them clothes that we could no longer wear, and a little food from our superfluity, and thereby do good to our souls.

I can see myself, a small, self-satisfied Pharisee, going down the road one frosty day with a pair of my discarded boots under my arm, and thinking myself a good many removes nearer Heaven as I walked back again with the grateful mother's praises sounding in my ears ; and perhaps I was, too. But I cannot have been very far advanced in saintliness, after all, for I know that when I saw the boots on the feet of one of the Lenaghan boys a few days later, neatly clouted by his father in his scanty evening leisure, I was heartily vexed that I had suggested their being given away.

On the whole I recall the little Lenaghans as objects of my envy. I envied them their freedom from the restraints of propriety and social observance. I envied them their exemption from the brushing of teeth, and the trimming of finger-nails, and the— to me—excessive use of soap. I washed with reluctance in those days, even though I knew and detested how my nostrils would smart when my face was washed for me. I had a natural affinity for dirt, just as much as the little Lenaghans had, and I envied their unrestrained liberty to practise it. In particular I envied their exemption from the use of pocket-handkerchiefs and the consequent necessity of keeping them clean. I often emulated their larger freedom in the matter of nose-blowing ; but somehow I never could quite acquire the trick of it, and desisted regretfully in the end, confessing to myself that the little Lenaghans were more highly gifted than I. Sartorially I envied them their emancipation from caps—and I might well do so, for I am sure that any one of them that is living has more hairs on his head than I—and their use of mufflers instead of collars, and their bare feet and callous soles in summer-time, and their reckless exposure of their nether garments to rents, and their subsequent fine disregard of protruding shirt-tails. In the article of gloves I rather thought I had the better of them. True, I hated wearing gloves ; but they were an acknowledged mark of social superiority ; and when I went past their house on my way to church on Sundays I always pulled on my gloves ostentatiously, and felt that I predominated over the little Lenaghans.

Then I envied them the knowledge of wild birds and wild flowers and insects that seemed almost intuitive to them, but was a constant mystery to me ; for I was a town-bred child for some years. All I know of woodcraft I learned from them ; and I wish I had been a more attentive pupil. Later I tried to make up my deficiencies from books ; but knowledge gained that way has not the same savour, and does not so dwell in the memory, or become part of oneself. To this day a yellowhammer is a " yellow-yorlin " to me, and a chaffinch an " apple-picker," and a newt a " man-creeper," a wicked insect that if you fall asleep by a waterside crawls down your throat and exterminates you; and I envied the little Lenaghans their knowledge of these things and of a great many other arcana of Nature into which I could never penetrate. But above all I envied them a certain kind of coarse sugar with large, flat grains, that their mother bought, and that presented its most alluring appearance when sunk in butter on the top of a split half-farl of soda-bread. And that is another source of envy that I had quite forgotten; for the little Lenaghans ate griddle-bread—when there was any—and our bread was baked in an oven, and wasn't the same thing at all. And, besides, they enjoyed another kind of bread compounded of oatmeal and potatoes —they called it " praitie-oaten "—and such a delectable viand was unknown in our house.

When I come to think of everything, the little Lenaghans can't have had such a bad time of it after all. For their father must have had more wages than nine pounds a year by my time, and he took his meals in our house, and had his cottage free —though it was the full rent it was worth—and free firewood, and milk and butter at a cheap uniform rate, and a rood of potato ground. No; decidedly the little Lenaghans had a better time of it than I recalled at first. And yet—and yet—I remember their father's face—and their mother's.

VICTUALS AND DRINK

In my young days the farm servants in Ulster always took their meals at the farm house. " Board-wages " were unknown, even for married men. The custom still obtains, but with the larger farmers it is fast dying out. The modern servant-girl will not endure it, and small wonder ; for under the system she was condemned to a life of endless drudgery, cooking and dish-washing. It is really she who has brought about the change ; for board-wages are abhorrent to the Ulster farmer, who, as a rule—like most farmers—does not care to part with ready money, and thinks he is keeping his wages-bill lower when he is paying part of it in kind.

But your modern country servant-girl is a shy bird, and even threatens to become extinct. She must be humoured or she will fly off to town or city service, and having tasted of the sweets thereof will never return to the slops of a country kitchen, or the foul ways of a farmyard in winter. She has become nice in her habits, dresses in a passable imitation of her mistress's imitation of fashionable garb, begins to insist, most unreasonably, on a night off in the week the same as her town sister, is known sometimes to possess a bicycle, and has generally, as my older country lady friends keep telling me, become much more " upsetting " than the girls they remember. To such an extent has she departed from common decency that I learn she has flatly refused lately to feed pigs, and demands that this unseemly office be delegated to some man kind. Her mistress is obliged to bow to the rod ; and in the kitchen presents an appearance of resignation if not of cheerfulness ; but when you call on your country friends, and Herself has looked cautiously out of the room and then closed the door, you hear sad tales of declension from the standard of " the servant girls of my day " ; and how " that blade in the kitchen is as big a lady as I am myself." To ask of such a damsel the unending slavery of indoor feeding of farm-hands is obviously out of the question ; and so " board-wages " are coming in.

The indoor system had its defects. For one thing it pressed hardly on the married ploughman's wife and children. He himself was sure of plentiful and nourishing food in most farmsteads ; but the residuary money wage was lamentably insufficient for his family's needs, in times gone by, at any rate. But from the farmer's point of view there were many advantages, the chief of which was that the master and his men were thrown into closer fellowship. They were more members of one family than employer and employed ; a keener sense of common aims and common interests possessed them. The servants were not the mere agents of their master's will. They took their part in shaping the destinies of the farm. If the master did not eat with his men he generally emerged from the Olympian aloofness of the " parlour " after the evening meal. The kitchen became a Parliament where questions of high policy were discussed ; whether the Barn Field should be broken up this year, or the Rush Meadow drained ; would the Hills bear cutting a second time, and was oats or flax the most likely crop for the Whinney Brae ; with a glance at such impending matters as the accouchement of the " springer " cow or the immolation of the fat porkers, whose evening meal the servant girl was at that moment making ready—no finicky modern miss in buckled shoes and a print dress, but a strapping, frowsy, red-armed wench, in clattering hob-nailed boots and a sack-cloth apron, or " rubber," as we called it, bustling about with a clash of zinc buckets, and driving even her master to hasty retreat from his own fireside with fear of scalded shins.

Under such a patriarchal system, while there was much more loyalty and *esprit de corps* among farm servants, there was naturally much less observance of outward forms of respect. In Leinster and Munster, farms are generally large ; and there is a distinct gap between master and man. Farm servants there will call their employer " sir," and even touch their hats to him ; a thing we do not hold with in the Black North, unless we are working for " the gentry." But farms in Ulster are much smaller.

In many cases farmer and hands sit at the same table, go afield together, and pick potatoes side by side in the same outhouse. In their working hours there is no social distinction between them. They will sit down amicably in the same ditch side to smoke a pipe together—literally " a pipe," for in the deficiency of tobacco I have seen one pipe do duty in alternate mouths with no greater sacrifice to ceremony than a perfunctory wipe of the mouthpiece on the seat of alternate trousers—and the servant's address to his master is simply " Robert," or " John," or " Thomas," as the case may be.

The dietary in my young days was plentiful, but rough, and roughly served. For breakfast there was set down a great tin dish of oatmeal porridge, made with water or buttermilk—it was called " paritch " in the vernacular ; the first time I saw the word " porridge " in print it savoured to me of literary affectation ; and the men supped them—for we called it " them "—out of tin mugs half-filled with sweet milk, and with iron spoons. After the porridge a mug of tea and a half-farl of home-made bread was handed each man ; and he drank his tea thankfully, even though he well knew it was " the room " tea with an extra spoonful thrown in on the used leaves, and well watered. For dinner there was boiled home-cured beef and bacon, mostly preceded by the broth in which it had been boiled, potatoes, and sometimes vegetables. On a Friday, if there were Roman Catholic servants, a couple of herrings, fresh or salted, took the place of the beef, and I have seen a half-dozen men sit contentedly enough round a table on which a potful of boiled potatoes had been emptied out steaming in their jackets, and make a meal on them with the accompaniment of only butter and sweet milk. The evening meal was the same as the morning one ; but sometimes the tea was brought out to the fields about four o'clock, and the day wound up with porridge.

We have become luxurious in the North now, I am told. Bacon and eggs are not unknown for breakfast ; in fact, labour impudently demands that they shall not be unknown. I have even heard of pudding for dinner ; but I cannot believe that. It would be a sore trial to my aunt, I know, if she were still alive. She had her own notions of how the lower orders should feed. The lower orders were aware of them.

A wandering mendicant used to call at our house occasionally, hoping for money, but generally put off with a meal. One day—there had been a party the evening before—my aunt stupefied him by setting before him a plate of chicken. He did not begin to eat it at once, and my aunt, thinking he was abashed by her presence, left the kitchen. As the door closed, the old fellow leaned over to the servant. " Biddy," he whispered cautiously, " Biddy, *what happened to the hin ?* "

BURNS IN ULSTER

I

THE country folk of Ulster are not much given to literature. Even in the towns we are content to subsist on scandalously short commons in the way of reading matter. It was but the other day I was reproached with the scarcity of book-shops in Belfast, and could only retort irrelevantly with the output of linen. True, we have taken no contemptible part in the Irish Literary Revival of recent years. Some of the sweetest singers among our latter-day poets are Ulster born and bred; and the accomplishment of the Ulster Literary Theatre alone would justify us in claiming our share in the restoration of Irish drama to truth and naturalness. But the field of culture is restricted. The bulk of the people, in town and country, remain as unliterary as ever. The Gaelic revival has not touched us, at least one section of us. That section will have no truck with Maeve and Grania, Cuchullin and Conchobar, the Fianna and the Children of Lir. It looks upon these fabled beings as having their origin not in Ireland, but somewhere among the Seven Hills; and is inclined to suspect them of a past not wholly untainted with the heresy of Home Rule. I do not think they will ever resume their sway in Ulster while the present population endures. They are too airy and unsubstantial for our Northern imaginations.

I was reared in the Lowland Scottish tradition of homely realism, and my Gamaliel was, strangely enough, a Celtic Irishman, one Paddy Haggarty, a servant on my aunt's farm. Paddy was a quiet, modest little fellow, not dull, for he had a pawky mother-wit, but not much given to speech, and taking no part in the rough horse-play that passed for humour among his fellows. I was a diffident child, a little spoiled by loneliness and too much reading, and over-sensitive to jests ; and Paddy and I struck up a friendship. He slept in a small apartment off the stable, and after he had tested me sufficiently he admitted me to the intimacy of his chamber, a privilege never before accorded to any person about the farm. The first few nights passed pleasantly enough. Paddy had an extensive fund of country anecdote ; and I unloaded on him the accumulations of some years of miscellaneous browsing among books, most of which I only partially understood. Though I failed to profit by Paddy's lessons in the art of smoking, I made some progress in taking snuff. But the real glory of our friendship dates from the night when Paddy, after shuffling in silence on his stool for a long time, asked me suddenly, " If I knew anything of Rabbie

Burns at all ? " I answered that I knew nothing of him save the name ; but that I had often intended to read his poetry, only there was not a copy in our house. To this day I can remember the almost reverent expression with which Paddy drew the dumpy little duodecimo volume from beneath his pillow. That night the harness-room Burns club was inaugurated.

For a long period I was content to fulfil the part of congregation at our worshippings, and remain a listener while Paddy read and expounded. I remember that he began with " The Twa Dogs," and how the friskings of our own collie and mastiff rose before my eyes as he read. Till then my acquaintance with verse had been restricted to Pope's *Homer*. This I encountered in an old-fashioned edition, in which the " s's " were printed as " f's," or so they seemed to me. They puzzled me a good deal. I never could understand what the dart meant by " hiffing on " before it " stretched in the dust the great Iphitus' son " ; but I accepted the reading without question, and the dart continued to " hiff " for me during many years. But I had read Pope for the bloodshed rather than for the poetry ; and this was a new kind of poetry that Paddy was reading me. The note of sincerity touched even my childish heart ; the homely dialect words sounded kindly in my Ulster ears. " Twa dogs that were na thrang at hame." From that line onwards I listened with all my soul ; and when the poem was finished I had become with Paddy a devotee in the worship of Rabbie Burns.

In general Paddy was sparing of commentary, and such exposition as he indulged in was apt to be coloured by his political opinions. When, for instance, he read in " The Twa Dogs " of the " poor tenant bodies, scant o' cash, How they maun thole a factor's snash," he paused to explain that a factor was, with us, a land-agent. " And, God knows," he added heartily, " the people of this counthry had plenty to thole from them, too, before Billy Gladstone's time." But I was rapt in the discovery that " thole " and " snash " were real words, and that I might use them in the future without shamefacedness ; and Paddy's agrarian bitterness passed by unheeding ears.

As became a younger disciple, I accepted without question Paddy's selections from the inspired text. His favourites were mine, and with a few exceptions they have remained so. To Paddy as a ploughman perhaps the " Address to a Mouse " had the more intimate appeal ; but I never had the heart to kill a field-mouse after. The homely truth of " The Farmer's Salutation to his Auld Mare Maggie," " The Death and Dying Words of Poor Mailie," and " Hallowe'en," charmed us both equally. We both assented heartily to the imprecatory " Address to the Toothache," and even thought we derived some benefit from the use of it as an incantation, such triumphs has faith. Neither of us knew what a " haggis " was, but I am sure that had one been placed before us we would have partaken of it almost sacramentally. Together we shuddered over " Death and Doctor Hornbook " and the " Address to the Deil " ; but I think I was more openly sympathetic than Paddy to the kindly relentings in the closing stanza of the latter ; for Paddy was already in his bedchamber, and I had the dark yard to cross.

But " Tam o' Shanter " was and has remained my favourite. Not even endless repetition—and we repeated it endlessly—could abate one single thrill I enjoyed even while I trembled. To this hour I can see Paddy lower his book and look at me as he delivered with solemn impressiveness :

> That night, a child might understand
> The deil had business on his hand.

I feel still the stirrings among my hair. It was many a year before I could hear thunder after nightfall without a cautious glance round for His Majesty ; and even now I am easier on a country walk by night when I have put a running stream between me and the powers of darkness.

II

The poems of religious satire Paddy passed over in silence, probably out of consideration for my feelings, but partly, no doubt, because as a

Roman Catholic the Auld and New Lichts stood for him equally as darkness. But he was aware of the purpose of these poems. Looking back I seem to discern from his reference to them that he derived some such satisfaction from this fouling of the Protestant nest as a Protestant might be supposed to draw from Erasmus' *Praise of Folly* or Pascal's *Provincial Letters*. The Songs neither of us read much. Here again Paddy may have been considerate of me ; but he was a staid little fellow, and not much given to dalliance. The Bacchanalian poems of Burns, however, appealed to him strongly. Though Paddy could not fairly be called a heavy drinker it must be admitted that in the matter of porter he was prone to occasional steppings aside ; and thirsty, mellow, or repentant, his mood was reflected in our readings. When the convivial element began to predominate I knew that Paddy would shortly go on the spree ; and I knew, too, that when the spree was over we would read largely in Rabbie's penitential psalms. Paddy used them as a kind of moral soda-water just as the hapless author must have done. But, however effective they proved as a cure, as a preventative they failed utterly, and at last after an unusually heavy spree Paddy betook himself to " the clergy " and solemnly renounced drink. He did not renounce Burns though ; and it was with misgiving that I enjoyed his spirited delivery of " John Barleycorn," some months later. I was justified by the event ; for Paddy having occasion to go to the fair of C—— allowed himself to be persuaded by some casuist that lager beer was within the limits of his pledge, and was found that evening by a ganger of the local railway peacefully sleeping in the track of an oncoming train. I think at first he felt himself ill-used in this affair ; for I remember that he subsequently recited the stanzas ending :

> But if I must afflicted be
> To suit some wise design,
> Then man my soul with firm resolves
> To bear and not repine,

as one rather bowing beneath the visitation of Providence than suffering from his own errors ; but his remorse did not endure long ; for a few nights after he read me " Scotch Drink " with a good deal of gusto, remarking cheerfully at the close that " Rabbie was no reading for a Temperance man " ; and so far as I know he never renewed his pledge.

Although I worshipped at the shrine of his idol with at least as much fervour as Paddy, I began presently to decline somewhat from his pure mono-theism. Having tasted of the sweets of poetry I was not content with my first sip, but began to range further, and diligently ransacked my aunt's library for books of verse. I could never carry Paddy with me. Not only did he refuse to be tempted from his poetical faith, but he was even chary of subjecting himself to temptation. I

remember that in my browsings I fell a victim to
the nimble facility of the *Ingoldsby Legends*. But
Paddy would have none of them ; and after hearing
the " Jackdaw of Rheims," refused to listen further,
on the ground that though he was no bigot he couldn't
be expected to like Orange poetry. I confess that
on reading the poem again I sympathized with him,
and was so appalled by my failure in tact that I
abstained from the harness-room for a long time.

During this period of voluntary exile I unearthed,
to my great delight, Bloomfield's *Farmer's Boy*,
and hastened with it to Paddy as a peace-offering.
But Paddy made short work of Bloomfield. He
listened patiently enough till I came to the passage :

> O'er heaven's bright azure, hence with joyful eyes
> The farmer sees dark clouds assembling rise ;
> Borne o'er his fields a heavy torrent falls,
> And strikes the earth in hasty driving squalls.
> " Right welcome down, ye precious drops," he cries ;
> But soon, too soon, the partial blessing flies.
> " Boy, bring the harrows, try how deep the rain
>   Has forced its way ! "

then stopped me. " Tell me, Master Lynn,"
he said, " did ye ever hear a farmer talk like that ? "
I had to admit that I never did.

" That's where Rabbie has it over them all,"
he went on. " Rabbie's poetry is just like a labourin'
man's talk, only someway or another it lilts itself
into verses. Was this Bloomfield brought up to
the land ? "

I said he was. " Well, he got little good of his trainin'," said Paddy. " I'll hold ye Rabbie could ha' made a guess of how deep a shower of rain went into a turnip field without turnin' out a harrow an' a pair of horses."

But I shook Paddy badly with a little volume of Robert Fergusson's poems. I conducted my attack better than I knew then; for Paddy was a fervent admirer of " The Cotter's Saturday Night "; and I began with its perhaps greater original, " The Farmer's Ingle." I could see that the beautiful opening stanzas impressed him :

When gloming grey out o'er the welkin keeks. . . .

He listened to the end of the poem in silence, then took the book from my hand, and turned the leaves over discontentedly. " The man has got most of his words from Rabbie," he said at length ; " but there's no denyin' he handles them well."

Presently he came on the lines :

When Father Adie first pit spade in
The bonny yard o' ancient Eden
His amry had no liquor laid in
        To fire his mou'.
Nor did he thole his wife's upbraidin'
        For being fou'.

His bairns had a' before the Flood,
A langer tack o' flesh an' blood,
An' on mair pithy shanks they stood
        Than Noah's line ;
Wha still hae been a feckless brood
        Wi' drinkin' wine.

Paddy closed the book with a smile of triumph. " I doubt," said he, " he's only a narrow body after all."

From that night on he would hear no more of Fergusson, and always spoke of him afterwards as " that teetotaller." Nor could I tempt him with other strange gods. " No, Master Lynn," he would say, " Rabbie'll do for me. Rich or poor, drunk or sober, there's always somethin' in him to suit a body. He'll last me my time."

If Paddy is above ground in the County Down he is likely of the same opinion still. The Gaelic Revival has repopulated the other three provinces, and the glens and mountains of Ulster, with fairies and leprechauns, whose airy tongues syllable a new language that is also old. But round about my part of the world we still people the dark hours with material and Gothic shapes, and call, in his own speech, on the great enchanter, Rabbie Burns.

THE FIRST READING-BOOK

IT was as far as I remember about three weeks after the coming of Anne Blaney to my aunt's house as domestic servant that Paddy Haggarty began to read the Songs of Burns. A very short time afterwards I heard him one evening crooning over to a tune that must have been his own composing :

> Her face is fair, her heart is true,
> As spotless as she's bonnie, O ;
> The opening gowan wat wi' dew,
> Nae purer is than Nannie, O.

Hitherto the reading of Burns by Paddy and myself had been confined to the poems of country life, and the Bacchanalian ditties ; but from this time on we devoted ourselves, at the instance of Paddy, to the discreetly amatory verse. I was too young to understand the significance of the change. The song quoted above, which became Paddy's favourite, and was the only one to which I ever heard him give musical expression, afforded no clue to my childish understanding.

I can see Anne now, a quiet, motherly little body, with a slightly pock-marked face, neutral-tinted hair, and clear, honest grey eyes. She was afflicted with a passion for tidiness that was a sore trial to both her and me ; nevertheless I liked her from the first. But I should never have thought of comparing her to an opening gowan wet with dew. To me she seemed quite old. Looking back, I suppose she must have been about twenty-six. But she was staid beyond her years. I could not think of her as ever having been young. I am sure that not even Robert Burns would have thought of addressing her as Nannie ; and I know she wouldn't have liked it if he had. Yet she awakened romance in Paddy Haggarty's heart; and he hymned her in every variant of her prim name, and remained unabashed.

The other servants on the farm were more observant than I was, and it soon got about that Paddy Haggarty was Anne's " boy." I did not believe the story for a long time, and did not venture to speak to Paddy about it. But one day I came upon him embracing Anne at the back of a haystack. I remember I thought it a rather silly business, and was chiefly impressed by the fact that I saw Anne's hair looking untidy for the first time since she had come to live at our house. I was aware, however, that embracing was a recognized symptom in such cases, and from that time on took their courtship as a matter of course, and had no diffidence in inquiring from Anne shortly afterwards when she was going to marry Paddy. To my astonishment she began to cry, not violently, but in a quiet, restrained fashion. I think I must have had a sympathetic manner in those days ; for Anne dried her tears presently and said if I would go with her to her room she would tell me all about it ; and that I was a kindly, good child, and it was no wonder Paddy liked me.

I was greatly flattered by her confidence, and sat patiently on the bed while she cried a little more before beginning her story. Then she told me that she loved Paddy Haggarty. He was the only man that had ever laid a finger on her, or ever would do so ; but she could never marry him.

I was very much astonished and distressed to hear this, and sat for a long time cogitating on the reason, while Anne cried again. Then I remembered that Paddy sometimes drank too much porter, and I asked Anne if that was why she wouldn't marry him. But Anne said, No ; as far as she was aware all men drank porter, and she would be lucky if she got a man that took it so seldom as Paddy. Finally she dried her tears and put her handkerchief back in her pocket, telling me very plainly and simply she had never been taught to read and write, and that Paddy had a deal of learning and he was always reading poetry, and she knew he would never disgrace himself by marrying a wife who had no education. There was no use saying anything more about it. She had made up her mind, and thought she could thole. I asked her if Paddy knew she could not read or write, and she told me he did not, and that she would die rather than tell him. And she said she meant to pretend she did not care for him any more, but kept putting it off, for she found it very hard to do.

I was a good deal shocked by what Anne had told me ; for I thought it very likely she was right, and that Paddy would not marry a wife who had no education ; and I had learned from my lighter reading that to be crossed in love was the most dreadful thing could happen to any person. But I was rather glad she was so old ; for my sense of romance told me that but for this it would clearly be my duty to grow up quickly and marry her myself. Then I thought out another solution as I lay in bed that night, and fell asleep picturing Anne as the faithful foster-mother of my children after my young wife's piteous death. But in the morning I had a still brighter inspiration, and hurried down to the kitchen with a conscience refreshingly clear about my unwashed face to tell Anne the difficulty was solved. *I* would teach her to read ; I was sure I could if she would only work hard ; and I knew she would do so, that Paddy might marry her soon. I remember that Anne was not nearly so excited as I had expected, but looked at me in her sober way and said, not very hopefully, she would try her hand at it anyway. I remember, too, that she sent me back to wash my face. I thought it very ungrateful of her after all my meditated kindness, and wasn't quite sure whether I was doing the best thing for Paddy. But after breakfast my enthusiasm returned.

When I came home from school with a new First
Reading-Book for Anne in my pocket, I was so
impatient that I thought it would never grow dark.
For we had arranged that three nights a week
I was to lie awake and meet Anne in the kitchen
when everyone else had gone to bed, and the first
lesson was to take place that night.

I can still see the dim kitchen, with ghostly
shapes of hanging garments on the walls, and hear
the creaking crickets, and watch Anne's earnest
face in the candle glow. I remember the very words
of some of our first lessons. " The cat is on the mat.
Is it Sam or Pat ? Sam has a fat ram. Dan has a
bad pen." I observe a certain want of continuity in
the thought ; but both Anne and I were too much
wrapped up in our task to be conscious of it at the
time. How often we repeated those phrases I
cannot now compute, but it must have run far into
the hundreds ; for Anne was a slow pupil. But
I was too much elevated in my own conceit to be
other than patient with her. I went about in a glow
of self-righteousness, hugging my secret to my
heart, and exulted over Paddy as a father might
over his favourite son. Little dramatic romances
wove themselves in my brain ; how, for instance,
Paddy should be called away to visit his sick mother
just after Anne had learned to write, and how I
would instruct her in composing a love-letter to
him. Then I pictured Paddy's amazement and
delight when he would receive the letter, and how

c

he would hurry back and clasp Anne to his bosom, and bring her off to his home just in time to have their hands solemnly joined by his dying parent. I was a little disconcerted in this particular romance by remembering suddenly that Paddy was not aware of Anne's illiteracy, and so would not be surprised by her letter, and spent many an hour vainly trying to re-cast my story, as I have often done since with other stories; but I cannot recall whether I succeeded or not.

I know that the real story ended quite undramatically, as most real stories do; for just about the time Anne was promoted to words of two syllables Paddy proposed to her, and was accepted; and as far as I could find out there was never a word said about education at all. Nor did I inquire too closely into the matter. To tell the truth, Anne had been making a very poor hand of the two syllables. I had lost a little of my enthusiasm; and was beginning to find it very hard to keep awake of nights. But I cried heartily when she and Paddy were married and went away to County Antrim, where Paddy had got a situation as under bailiff on a gentleman's estate. Years later, when I learned about wedding presents, I sent Paddy a handsome edition of Robert Burns' poems. Later still, when I had learned the value of old friends, I went to visit the couple, and wasn't a bit disappointed to find my beautiful present enshrined in " the room," carefully dusted, but never opened.

Paddy still made use of the crabbed little duodecimo that he and I had read together many a night in the harness-room at home.

As we sat at tea Anne reminded me quite placidly of the nights when I had tried to teach her reading ; and Paddy and she smiled at the reminiscence, wandering on to talk of old times.   Then I saw that the disparity of education had never been thought of much between them, or troubled their happiness.

ODIUM THEOLOGICUM

IT is well known that in the North of Ireland we take our politics seriously ; and, since our politics and our religion are inextricably mingled, the same is true of our religion. On these two vital points some people think we are as bitter as ever. I am not certain about it. One dogma, maintained equally firmly by Catholic and Protestant when I was a boy —the eternal damnation of all adherents of the opposite faith—is being considerably impaired by the lapse of time. We are as sure as ever we were that we are right and that our opponents are wrong ; but about the exact consequences of their error we are less positive than we used to be.

A story is told of a well-known Presbyterian divine who flourished in Ulster many years ago. After exhorting a backslider among his flock long, earnestly—and vainly—he raised his clenched fist— it was no small one—"You'll go to hell," he thundered. " You'll go to hell as surely as I'll crush that fly." The fist descended ; but the insect avoided fate, and buzzed away unharmed. The chagrined minister silently followed its flight. "Well, well," he said at length, reluctantly, I am afraid, though he was a good man, " the Lord is merciful and long-

suffering. There may be a chance for you yet."
About our opponents in religion we begin in the
North, perhaps equally reluctantly, to be of the
reverend gentleman's opinion. There may be a
chance for the other fellow, we think.

But when I was a boy there was no such sentimental tampering with the decrees, as we undestood them,
of a just Providence. Damnation, utter and final,
was the lot of the goats ; and we were the sheep
always.

About ninety-five per cent. of the scholars at the
country school I attended till the age of eleven
were of the opposite creed to mine. We of the five
per cent. were under no delusions about the eternal
future of the ninety-five, nor did the disparity in
numbers ever prevent us from making our convic-
tions manifest. I bear in my head records of our
long controversy, principally caused by well-aimed
road metal. It was at the close of secular instruction
for the day, that war most frequently broke out.
The majority suffered daily half an hour's religious
instruction after we were free to depart, and we
used to linger a while to emphasize—indiscreetly—
our advantage.

As we made our *post-bellum* journey home,
we often discussed with mingled awe and contempt
what fearful rites were practised during that mysterious half-hour. I am sure the reality fell far short
of our dark surmises. One of the hardier spirits
among us nearly achieved initiation once by scaling

a window. It was felt to be a perilous mission. The rest of us watched from a safe distance, poised for flight. But almost in the very moment of success the adventurer's toe slipped out of the too shallow chink we had secretly cut in the wall, and an abraded knee and a bitten tongue persuaded him that there should be no traffic with the unclean thing.

He was helped to this conviction next day by our Master, who had marked his disordered flight. An upright, conscientious man, the Master would have been years ahead of his age if he had been any less sure of our ultimate damnation than we were of his. Yet he always dealt more than justice to the minority lest he might be suspected of bias. On this occasion he would have been more than human had he spared the rod; for certainly it was in no spirit of reverence that Johnny D—— drew near his ministrations.

Once only did I know the Master to display something of the North of Ireland Adam. The warmer controversialists had hit on a device for conducting their disputes even during school hours. One young zealot would chalk on his slate—I blush to relate it—" To H—— with the Pope," and exhibit the legend for an instant, at the same time projecting over the slate a contorted visage with thrust-out tongue ; to which his opponent hastened to retaliate by exhibiting in the same manner, " To H—— with King William." Unluckily for the Romanist champion on a certain occasion, the Master, turning in his quarter-deck pacing, a couple or so yards short of his recognized mark, caught him in the very act of proclaiming his faith. Instantly he pounced on him, dragged him by the ear, squirming, to his desk, and drew forth his cane. To this day I can recall the deficiency of my saliva as I strove hastily to obliterate my own pious aspirations for the reigning Pontiff.

" Rub out that disgraceful sentence, sir," roared the Master to the discovered culprit. " And now, Joseph," he continued with the inflection of sorrow that all of us dreaded and none of us believed in, " I regret that I shall have to cane you soundly. But first I must tell you how hurt and pained I am to find you writing such a sentence on your slate. A Catholic should not be guilty of such an action. It's unmannerly, and unchristian, and"—he was thought to have a turn of wit, and the temptation was too much for him—" *unnecessary*."

It was in this atmosphere that I was born and brought up, nor has the air greatly cleared since then. Yet none but an Ulster man can fairly criticize Ulstermen. The foreigner, looking at the surface of things, judges both sides too hardly. There was a good deal of convention in our attitude towards one another in those days, as I think there is still. In theory we hated one another bitterly, but practice did not follow at theory's heels, in country districts at least. Our childish freaks apart, in all my boyhood I never knew of anyone being insulted on account of his religion, or beaten, or injured in his property or business. I never knew a man refuse to give employment on that account, or turn away a servant—or buy in a dearer market. These things may have been done in the towns—doubtless all of them were, except the last—but in the country I never knew an instance of them. About festival times, the Twelfth of July and the Fifteenth of August, there was a good deal of tall talk ; the flame of zeal burned higher for a space before and after these seasons ; but the two parties never came to blows in our district. I once saw blood spilt at the Twelfth of July ; but it was over a matter of precedence between two Orange Lodges, when in the fraternal conflict John Simson, a noted drummer, was grievously smitten with a flute.

We possess in the North one great corrective of bitterness, that dry sense of humour that is so often infused with self-criticism. We are conscious of our bitterness, and see the ridiculous side of it now and then. In a strange way it is a bond of union between the two parties. I have heard a knot of Ulstermen of both sides, thrown together at an election or a lawsuit outside their native province, beguile a whole evening with apt anecdote of their mutual feud ; and the shrewdest knocks were often self-inflicted. There is hope for the future in such an attitude of mind, when " our follies, turning round against themselves, in support of our affections, retain nothing but their humanity."

When I mix in such a gathering I see that the true solvent of our *odium theologicum* is mutual intercourse. I esteem it fortunate that I was educated for some years at a mixed school. It does not seem, as I have described it, a nursery of toleration ; but seeds of toleration were sown there. When you go to school with your enemy, you are in the way to becoming his friend. The black-eye I received at the hand of Peter H——over a point of dogma, thirty years ago, is a tie between us nowadays when we meet. We differ on that point of dogma still ; but Peter will never blacken my eye about it again, nor wish to do so. We know each other, and estimating our differences, find them outweighed by friendship.

I had other such advantages in my upbringing whereby the root of bitterness has failed to flourish in my soul. The priesthood visited little at Protestant houses when I was a boy, and would not have been very warmly greeted if they had done so ; but old Father B—— and my Cousin Joseph liked and respected each other, and the old man was a welcome guest at my cousin's house. I often met him there, and so lost my childish dread of his cloth. Not even a little Ulster boy could have been afraid of old Father B——. Even my aunt, when speaking of him, went so far as to say that " there was good and bad of all sorts." He used to give me pennies, and when his ramshackle phaeton with the old white pony in it overtook me on the road to school he never failed to help me on my way. Perhaps I would have been happier on foot. I felt my orthodoxy a little blown upon on the days when Father B——drove me to school. On such days I was a keener partisan of the Protestant faith than usual. But this aggravation of zeal was only outward show. In secret my bigotry was being undermined by Father B—— and his pennies, and his pony-phaeton, and his white hair and kind old face. I was never in danger of becoming a proselyte to his faith, nor did he ever try to make one of me ; but without knowing it he planted a little seed of toleration in my Ulster soul. Years after he stretched out his hand from the grave to water it·

When my Cousin Joseph died it fell to my lot to assist in sorting his papers, of which he had left a great many, being a kindly man to whom a friend's letter was a precious thing. In the corner of a wooden box I found a parcel of letters wrapped up in an old newspaper. A marked passage in the newspaper recorded a presentation to the Protestant clergyman under whom my Cousin Joseph had sat—as our Northern phrase goes. I knew him well, a genial man and a tolerant, as befitted a bosom crony of my Cousin Joseph's. I knew, too, that he had shared my cousin's like for old Father B——. I had watched the pair smoke a pipe together many an evening. So I was not greatly surprised to find among the bundle of letters—which related to the presentation—one from Father B—— to my Cousin Joseph. It ran something like this :

" MY DEAR JOSEPH,

"I hear you are getting up a presentation to my old friend, the Rev. Mr. N——. You did not ask me to contribute. I can quite well understand why, though I think, my dear Joseph, you might have known me better. But I hope you will allow me to give something towards it. For the Rev. Mr. N—— is my friend, and a man of peace, which I think every Christian clergyman should be."

When I looked at the list of contributors I saw that my Cousin Joseph had accepted Father B——'s contribution. It was not the smallest in the list.

To a reader born outside of the Ulster of my youth it might not have seemed a very remarkable thing that one Christian clergyman should wish to pay a mark of respect to another ; but I knew better. As I read Father B——'s letter the old man's face came back to me, and the face of his friend, and remembering that there were not many men of peace among the clergymen of those times I felt glad that I had been privileged to know two of them, and had found grace—though at some lapse of time—to profit thereby.

MY COUSIN WILLIAM

My Cousin William was an Ulster Presbyterian of the old school. It was in his company that I first became acquainted with the Presbyterian form of worship. I did not find the experience altogether pleasant. I was a shy child, and shrank from notoriety ; and when at the first prayer he stood up in his pew, turning his back on the Minister, I confess I was appalled. A scared glance round the church showed me that all the elder men were standing in like fashion. I perceived that it would be indecent to kneel. But I could not bring myself to follow my cousin's example. I felt that I should testify to the faith that was in me and refuse to stand up in the House of Rimmon. So I compromised ; and suffered the long prayer in a crouching posture, resolving that I would never again stray from my own fold. It was in a highly critical frame of mind that I straightened myself up for the following psalm. But I did not long preserve my aloofness. The simple rhythm of the metrical version as the minister read it out struck pleasantly on an ear not yet attuned to the subtler cadences of our own Prayer Book rendering. My curiosity was aroused by the faint breathing of a pitch-pipe sounding mysteriously from nowhere, and sharpened by the musical drone of the unmarked precentor as he hummed the key-note. Then with a stern vigour that thrilled my heart the psalm arose, strong, simple, unadorned ; and all my prejudices vanished. It was the forty-ninth psalm : " God is our refuge and our strength," and the tune was " Martyrdom." I had never heard such singing till then. There was an organ in our church ; our slender choir strove with it, but seldom prevailed, and we in the congregation left them to the unequal struggle ; but here everyone sang, men and women, girls and boys. Perhaps the result might not have pleased a more cultivated ear than mine. I still think my Cousin William would have been wiser not to sing. But I was moved by that psalm as I had never been moved by any music before. The ring of simple sincerity and defiant faith stirred echoes of old story. There was a rebel note in the strain. I was Henry Morton, and the high, stern hymn of enthusiasm floated towards me across the marshes of Drumclog. That psalm interpreted to me the spirit of Puritanism. The tradition in which I was brought up has more of colour and warmth and mystery. I would not willingly adopt any other. The light of eternity, when it reaches me at all, comes to me through stained glass windows, and floating on the wings of cunning music. But the creed of my Cousin William was worthy of his sturdier race, and more bracing to the soul.

Time has modified the ceremonial of Presbyterianism since my Cousin William's days. There is a harmonium in the little meeting-house now; and I am told they sometimes sing hymns. It is not for me to comment, much less to criticize; but my cousin would not have approved. For him the Psalms of David were the only fit vehicle of praise. He was very hardly persuaded to consent to paraphrases. It was a pious thought to bury him in a distant nook of the kirk-yard, out of sound of the instrument against which he so long contended. Measured by feeling he dwelt in a religious world nearer the sixteenth century than the twentieth. The ancient practice was unimpaired by time so long as he continued a ruling elder. When the congregation broke the memorial bread together it was in apostolic simplicity. The humble board stood on trestles in the aisle. The minister prayed in such words as came to him, or read a few sentences from that piteous story of long ago; the platter of bread went from hand to hand; the elders, passing round with a flagon, served the cup as Peter or John might have done in that Supper-room of nineteen centuries before. The worshippers ate their Sacramental meal reverently but composed, as men who looked not that their Lord should descend on them in the form of spirit, but rather take his place among them as Man. It is long years since I was present at the Presbyterian rite; it may be conducted differently nowadays; but I know that as a boy I witnessed it with emotion and tears.

Yet there was a certain matter-of-factness in their dealings with sacred things that from my training I could never attain to. I have been at a tea-party in a Presbyterian Meeting-house before now, but I would be well into the second cup before I began to relish my meal. I have often tried to enjoy the subsequent concert, and have sometimes succeeded ; but I was never quite at ease. If the roof had fallen in at any moment it would only have been what I was looking for. But such a state of mind was nothing to what I experienced the first time I attended Cousin William's Meeting-house on Sacrament Sunday, when as we drove home together he produced from his pockets a square of the species of short-cake used at the solemn table, telling me with a benevolent smile it was a portion that had been left over. I did not dare to refuse the offered fragment ; but I took it very much as some timid member of his band must have received the Shew Bread under the commanding eye of King David ; and my flesh crept as I ate.

But if there was little of the mystical in my Cousin William's religion it was an ever-present reality to him. His garment of righteousness was no ceremonial vestment to be put on and laid aside at sundry appointed hours and times ; it was his daily raiment. His faith was childlike and unquestioning, troubled by no introspective pryings, enfeebled by no casuistries of doubt. Nor was he given to spiritual pride. His confidence was rooted in humility. He knew himself a sinner, and was *therefore* assured of his salvation.

For an Ulster Protestant of his generation he was tolerant, though for the eternal welfare of his Roman Catholic neighbours he looked perhaps more to the mercy of their Creator than to the efficacy of their faith. Yet I have heard him say more than once that he did not see why the Pope should not be a good man. He was practical, too, in his toleration. It was his boast that he had never made the difference of a shilling between a Protestant and a Catholic in his life.

He had his prejudices; but he was slow to carry them to the point of interference with others. A fanatical teetotaller in theory and practice, I have know him to abstain from the Bench—for he was of the Quorum—when his neighbour Barney D——'s licence was in annual question. He would be glad, he said, to have the house closed, but he could not see his way clear enough to justify him in taking the bread from a neighbour's mouth.

His pleasures were few and simple, and seldom led him beyond his orbit as a farmer. He loved a neat homestead, and delighted in whitewash and red-lead. His hedges were trim to a fault. Round about his dwelling they were his personal care; and there fancy blossomed in him. The garden hedge was adorned with strange shapes of birds and beasts, a little stiffer, perchance, than Nature would have chosen ; but she was never able to steal a march on his shears.

He was handy with his clasp-knife, too. A whole army of fierce little soldiers, with bright red coats and bright blue trousers, stood to attention on sticks all round the house, and brandished their wooden swords fiercely in every breeze. The one in the front garden was my special favourite. He was more embellished than the others, in honour of his post of dignity. His red coat was adorned with blue buttons, and his blue trouser-legs had each a red stripe. His countenance was perhaps more striking than beautiful. His broad cheeks were very red, and his eyes very blue. My cousin used to say whimsically that he was an ugly fellow like himself ; and though I didn't think my Cousin William ugly at all, I felt in my heart there was a resemblance.

There was a patriarchal simplicity in my Cousin William's way of living. He rose with the lark, and lay down with the lamb. He was fond of telling in his old age that he had never seen the lamps of B—— lighted. He was more the father of his servants than their master. After the evening meal he moved to the kitchen, and sitting in his great arm-chair—my cousin was a large man—put on his spectacles and read the daily paper to his house-keeper and his men. His comments on politics were coloured with a cautious Radicalism. He did not love landlords, and had been a great tenant-

D

right man in his day. But on the question of
Home Rule he was what in Ulster would be called
" sound." He admired Gladstone ; but thought
his reforms should have stopped at the Land Acts.

When his early bedtime drew near he reached
down from the cupboard the Bible and his book
of Family Worship, and we had prayers. I always
remained for prayers on a night when I was
visiting there. I felt more secure when crossing
the bogs afterwards. The Protestant men-servants
used to remain, too ; in many cases, no doubt, from
a sense of piety, but not in all. I knew quite well
that John H——, his yard-man, had no such motive.
John always fidgeted on his knees and prayed with
his pipe in his hand. I am afraid he caused sad
wandering in my thoughts. Our little ceremony
closed with the Lord's Prayer. By that time John's
pangs had become almost insupportable ; I knew
quite well he would grope for a match about " De-
liver us from evil," and though I closed my eyes
reverently at the beginning of the prayer I always
looked through my fingers then, in a kind of
wager with myself whether I would hit the actual
moment. I confess, too, that—little sinner that I
was—some peculiarities of my cousin's did not
escape my magpie observation even in that solemn
hour. I early observed that in conducting the
service he fell into unconscious imitation of his
worthy minister in manner and diction. Even in
his pronunciation I caught echoes of the Meeting-

house pulpit. The good clergyman, among other idiosyncrasies of speech, commonly, I remember, said " gresshously hear us," and " O Gud," and my cousin faithfully copied these peculiarities in his own ministerings. The variations took my fancy the first time I heard family prayers in my Cousin William's, and I tried them in my own private devotions that night. But on reflecting in the dark I was convicted of levity, and clambered out of bed in the cold, and said my prayers over again.

But my Cousin William did not know the wickedness of my heart. I was a favourite of his. He thought me a good child ; and indeed his influence made me so. When I was in his company I turned my best side outward.

It was not from hypocrisy, either. I loved my Cousin William, and respected and looked up to him more than to any other man I have known before or since. He was a little old-fashioned in his notions ; the scope of his mind was not very wide ; he would have liked the thing that shall be to remain the thing that has been, and such an attitude does not make for progress. But he was simple, and good, and kind. If his creed was narrow his heart was big, and it was by the dictates of his heart that he steered his course in life. He was a shrewd man, too, within his limitations, and had a certain homely pithiness of speech, and could be angry for the right as he saw it. He stood for my conception of Doctor Johnson after my childish reading of Boswell ; and though I smile now, it may be that the great Doctor, looking to essentials as he always did, would not have disdained the comparison.

If my Cousin William had any weakness it was that he was a little too fond of land. Had I been the Adversary and my Cousin William enacting the part of Job, I would have assailed him on the tenth commandment, with a few acres of good meadow. Yet he would have prevailed against me. He made wide his boundaries while he lived, but died with the blessing of the widow and the fatherless.

He was a frugal man, but leaned more to saving than to getting, and did not make haste to grow rich. In the cause of charity or of religion he could be nobly generous, without self-righteousness. There was a heartiness in his bounty that multiplied the gift. Nor did he lack the grace of small benevolences. I had gone to boarding-school before he died ; and when I said good-bye to him at the end of the holidays he always gave me a shilling, and patted me on the head and told me to be a good boy and mind my task. The last time I said good-bye to my Cousin William he was sitting by himself in his parlour. He was as kind and cheerful as ever, but a little graver. We had a long, quiet chat together ; and he told me about the days when he, too, was a boy. He had not been quite so well lately, he said ; and being confined to the house a good deal had fallen to thinking of old times. But I wasn't to say anything at home about his illness ;

for people had their harvest to mind. When I bade him good-bye he held my hand longer than usual, and prayed God to bless me and make me grow up a good man. I looked in my palm after I had left the room, and saw he had given me half a sovereign. It was a great sum of money to me then; but I was not elated by my good fortune, and walked home very soberly across the bogs.

DRUMS AND FIFES

To an Ulster boy brought up in a district where the two parties, Nationalist and Orange, were almost equal in numbers, and political feeling consequently strong, the name of a Home Ruler had necessarily a sinister sound. Home Rulers to my childish mind were a dark, subtle, and dangerous race, outwardly genial and friendly, but inwardly meditating fearful things. I knew that when the signal was given, and one never could tell the moment, they were ready to rise, murder my uncle, possess themselves of his farm, and drive out my aunt and myself to perish on the mountains. It was some miles from our farm to the mountains. I used to wonder dimly how we should be able to make our way thither at such a time. But in my aunt's stories it was on the mountains we always died, and I felt that we were bound to get there somehow.

Looking back, it seems strange to me that both my aunt and myself should have tacitly exempted from our ban those Roman Catholics—for in my youth Roman Catholic and Home Ruler were synonymous terms—with whom we came into close personal relations. To me Paddy Haggarty, our second ploughman, was simply Paddy Haggarty. I took it as a matter of course that he should go to Mass on Sunday mornings, and eat fish on a Friday; and attributed no particular turpitude to him on account of these things. As for my aunt, I know that in matters demanding honesty and fidelity she would have trusted Tom Brogan, her thirty years' retainer, sooner than the Worshipful Master of an Orange Lodge.

Nevertheless, the unknown Home Ruler remained to me an object of fear and suspicion, hateful as an individual, but in association an incubus. The United Irish League was at that time the body through which Celtic Ireland sought political regeneration, and the League Rooms were as abominable to me as the Temple of Dagon to a devout Israelite of old. Even in the daytime its green shutters had a sinister look. I would not willingly have gone past the building after nightfall.

How I laughed not long ago to hear our little Roman Catholic maid plead to be excused from an evening errand that would have led her past the neighbouring Orange Lodge. It was Lodge night, she said, and she wouldn't go near the place for anything. But the incident illuminated my childhood. I saw that many a little Catholic, side by side with whom I had trotted to school in outward friendliness and inward mistrust, must have felt towards me just as I did towards him. The pleasant yellow of the Orange Hall shutters that smiled so reassuringly upon me, must to him have glimmered malignantly through the mists of inveterate tradition.

Yet there was little of which he need have been afraid. I have never been an Orangeman ; but as a child I associated a good deal with Orangemen, and dwelt on the very fringe of their mystery. In my tender years the Twelfth of July was a sacred festival, and the procession a solemn rite. I tended the Orange lilies in our garden very much as the Roman Vestals must have nourished the sacred birds, and on the Eleventh night made oblation of them with swelling heart for the annual Arch under which Protestant and Catholic passed to and fro all the next day, doubtless with some diversity of emotion.

Our first ploughman, William Brown, put on something of the pontifical with his Orange sash as he went forth on the Twelfth morning. I remember yet my thrill when the tossing banners first gleamed yellow among the distant trees ; and when at the road end, holding tightly to my nurse's hand, I watched the procession pass, the corybantes of fife and drum, whom I had known yesterday as mortal men and neighbours, were become a priesthood. Presently, as I grew stronger in the legs and was allowed to walk to the field of assembly in a lucky year when it was near at hand, I began to abate something of my awe. Carnal imaginings of cakes and ginger-ale began to mingle in my anticipations of the Twelfth. I began to lose my dread of big drums as I encountered them piled inglorious on the field, and even to essay a sacrilegious thump at one now and then on the sly. Something of respect and wonder they still inspired ; but it was as merely mortal instruments. I imbibed legends of their acoustic powers ; how a drum with one head made of ass's skin rose super-eminent in sound above ordinary drums, but drums with two such heads were forbidden by law, such was their window-shattering might. A spirit of the virtuoso dawned in my mind. I began to perceive some evidences of design amid the welter of noise, to discern fine points of drumming. And then our neighbouring lodge formed a flute and drum band ; and big drums fell from their high estate for ever. Henceforward for me Orangeism connoted music. I longed to become an Orangeman ; but it was as a musician, and no longer as a martyr in a great cause The possibility was now not utterly unthinkable. Quite small boys, I saw, were allowed to play the triangle. After one or two experiments with saucepan lids I even began to dream of the cymbals. But the ultimate reality was glorious beyond my imagining. My aunt became aware of my yearnings, bestowed upon me her blessing and a " D " flute, and set me off one morning with William Brown to be enrolled in the band.

It would be too long to tell of my initiation and progress ; my timid entry into the sacred precincts ; the momentary return of my former awe as I marked the tattered flags hanging from the roof, the skeletons of time-worn drums, the mysterious regalia in its tabernacle of glass ; of my wrestlings with the high " G " in " Killarney," and how the suave melody in " La Somnambula " stole into my soul ; of my thrill almost to pain when I first heard the four short crescendo rolls in the penultimate phrase of " The British Grenadiers," and how in consequence thereof I deserted the flute for the kettledrum.   In one way it was not an unprofitable time. I cannot play the flute now ; and when but yesterday I essayed to renew the glories of the kettledrum— on a tin can—for my youngest son, my " roll " was a thing of naught.   But all was not loss.   I can look back now and recall, not the band of furious zealots eager to wade knee-deep in blood, that our neighbours were taught to see in us, but a body of soberminded, earnest youths and men, cherishing a simple loyalty to " those put in authority over them " that often conflicted with their own material interests; holding firmly to principles that they perhaps imperfectly understood, but for which many of them would have cheerfully died ; in theory detesting the religious tenets of the majority of their fellowcountrymen, but in practice kind and neighbourly without distinction of faith, and in their own place of assembly yielding to that very charm of rite and vestment that was so incomprehensible to them in the ceremonies of others.   I like to think that had I been privileged to enter the rallying-room of

United Irishism I should have found there also nothing worthy of hate or dread, that I need no more have trembled to pass the temple of my little schoolmate's childish political faith than he to pass mine. I remember, too, that in the bond of common craftsmanship our big drummer, Bob J——, came closer to Barney H——, the drummer of the " Young Erin " band, than he did to any Protestant in Ulster ; and dare to hope greatly for the future from that touch of Nature, working in nobler things.

Who shall appraise the value of common aims, and common interests, and common memories; of mutual knowledge, when we have discarded our blind guides, and know one another as we are, not as we are feigned to be. Who knows but my little friend's grandson and mine may some day stand hand in hand with swelling bosoms when the drums break forth, and Orange and Green come down the road together in memory of dead Irishmen who fought in diverse causes, and sometimes with one another, but always for Ireland.

A NIGHT WALK

As a boy I enjoyed a reputation for hardihood, in my Cousin Joseph's family. When I set out of a dark winter's night for the lonely two-mile walk home, no one ever thought of offering to accompany me. I marched off whistling, proudly conscious of the half-scared, half-admiring faces of the little cousins, my contemporaries, who clung around the door-cheeks and peered fearfully into the night. Cousin Joseph never failed to say I was a plucky fellow; and his children's quavering farewells testified still more eloquently to my courage. As far as might be I lived up to my reputation with them. If water had to be fetched from the well after nightfall, or old John the yardman summoned from his lonely " sleeping-house " away at the end of the farmstead, I was always the one to volunteer for duty. When ghosts were timidly hinted at among us my voice was always high in derision— till an hour or so before my departure for home. After that time I played for safety; and if I did not confess I was at least careful not to blaspheme.

The truth is, that night walk was a horror to me. From the moment that Cousin Joseph's hall door cut off light, and strange tree-shapes leaped up

menacing before me, I scarcely drew a natural
breath till I reached the ash tree at the foot of our
avenue. At that point I always took to my heels.
Till then I kept myself in hand, and at dangerous
spots walked slower than my usual. If I quickened
my pace my courage declined. I felt myself in
danger of running ; and I knew that if I once ran
it was all over with me. I would be delivered into
the power of the Adversary, and become the quarry
in an infernal hunt of which the end was madness or
perhaps death. But at the ash-tree our kitchen
door was within the limits of a single effort ; and
the impulse to lay hold on safety was always too
strong for me. Besides, a little watercourse ran
under the road there. But it was a tiny trickle at
best. I was never quite sure of its efficacy except
in rainy weather ; and for the most part I put my
trust in speed. How well I remember that sobbing
rush, and my creeping scalp, and the icy breath that
struck between my shoulders. Then the struggle
to regain calm that my knock might be unhurried,
the endless moment of waiting, the glad sound of
scraping chair and clumping feet, and the shudder
as I crossed the threshold.

Not that I was a greater coward than any other
child of my age, but my knowledge was more.
Few children knew the ghostly topography of that
journey as I did. For the first half-mile or so there
was nothing more than such stuff for the imagination
as any country road could furnish of a dark night,

a misshapen bush, a wandering goat, a cottier's belated washing. Such sources of the supernatural are not to be despised. It is a poor sheet that cannot find some shivering spirit glad enough to clothe his nakedness with it ; and many a ghost that holds its head high in the underworld is sprung from nothing more alarming than a stray goat with a dragging chain. But my homeward road had no need of such impostors. For the last mile and a half it was thronged with authentic spirits.

I knew too well the little bank where Tom Hillis had died of a surfeit of whiskey on his way home from B——races. He sat there every night at the hour when his tipsy spirit had departed. But no one had been present at his death ; and who was to say when the spot might not be tenanted ? I shut my eyes before I came to that part of the road ; and if he was ever sitting there when I passed I was spared the knowledge.

At the first cross-roads William Dornan the highwayman had been buried with a stake through his heart, long before my time, for blowing out his brains when he was surrounded by his pursuers, instead of allowing himself to be brought to Belfast and hanged like a Christian. William was a merely historic ghost, picturesque but unconvincing. I had disinterred him from a local memoir and given him to the countryside again. But I was never able to bestow on him even spiritual substantiality. The statute of limitations had run for William ;

nobody regarded him seriously ; I wasn't very much afraid of him myself.

It was another matter with the Tinker's Wife. The memory of her dreadful end still lingered in the countryside. I have spoken with old men who had seen her husband and murderer executed. The precise spot where she died had become a little uncertain by my time. At any part of the tree-shaded quarter of a mile beyond the cross-roads one might meet the couple, he stalking moodily a few yards in front of his victim, as they walked in life. That quarter of a mile I went softly, treading on the grassy margin of the road, my ears strained for the thin clash of tinware.

After that the oak on which Blind James had hanged himself remained to be passed. But Blind James had been considerate of little boys in his end. The fatal tree was full two hundred yards from the road. Of a moonlight night, it is true, his pendulous form was plain to be seen. But it is still a matter of faith to me. I never tested the authenticity of the story by looking.

Last ordeal of all was the churchyard. No special legend of terror attached to it. For aught I knew its silent citizens had all been laid to rest with full rites, and patiently awaited judgment. But between midnight and cock-crow even the blessed dead might walk ; and I had small doubt that they exercised their privilege. It mattered little to me that I was never afoot in those hours. I could not

tell how time ran in Hades, or by what calendar
the clocks of eternity were set. I averted my face
during my long passage of the churchyard wall, and
thence onward avoided the error of Lot's wife.
It would have been wiser to look back. Ghost
after ghost took up its silent station at my shoulder.
By the time I reached my ash-tree the dread Trump
might have sounded over K—— churchyard and
awakened no more commotion than in a burial place
of Sadducees.

GHOSTS

It was in Robert Murray's that I had laid upon me my burden of ghostly knowledge; the last cottage in County Down one would have associated with the supernatural. A cheerful, almost rowdy, cottier's dwelling, filled to the brim with father and mother, half a dozen working sons, and two grown-up daughters, and running over nightly with casual droppers-in. Robert's was my favourite cottage to visit in of winter nights.· I liked to go there early and watch the womenfolk bustling over the preparation of the family supper. Perhaps hot griddle-cakes buttered, and of a lucky night sugared as well, had something to do with my preference. I had never eaten such griddle-cakes before. By telling my aunt that, one night, I nearly cut myself off from Robert Murray's fireside for ever. It was Mary Murray who baked the griddle-cakes. Hannah was the better-looking of the two sisters, and the livelier; but Mary was the more industrious, in spite of her delicate health, and had the kinder heart. I loved Hannah during the greater part of my tenth and eleventh years; but it was with a merely romantic passion. When I thought of marriage about that time it was always Mary I had in my mind.

A great deal of baking was necessary in Robert's house. From about seven o'clock steady eating set in ; good, plain, appetizing food ; endless farls of soda-bread and oat-cakes and potato-oaten, and tea in quarts, black and hot and strong, with three or four teaspoonfuls of sugar to every cup ; such tea as the sedentary worker does not drink with impunity after twenty-five. I look at the straw-coloured liquid I am condemned to nowadays, and sadden when I remember Mrs. Murray's rich, fragrant brew of one and a half teaspoonfuls to each adult, and one for the teapot. None of your cheap tea either. The best teas in the London market came to the North of Ireland, I have heard it said ; and the best of those were drunk in the labourers' cottages. No self-respecting cottier's wife paid less than three and sixpence a pound when I was a boy. I lived to see top-priced tea come down to half a crown. It was advertised as a special blend, too ; but Mrs. Murray wouldn't have believed in it.

Supper was a running meal at Murray's. The men of the family came in one after the other, according to the distance they had to tramp from their work, satisfied their hunger, and took their places by the fire. By the time dishes were washed and the womenfolk had " cleaned themselves " callers began to arrive. The kitchen door would open slowly just wide enough to admit a head and

shoulders. When the newcomer had surveyed the
company, and saluted them with a slow sideways
nod of the head, he would permit his legs to enter,
and then seat himself in silence and get out his
pipe. In about ten minutes he would be thawed
enough to join the conversation. By the time he
was amalgamated in the circle, another visitor
would have arrived, till about eight o'clock the
kitchen was half-filled with people and completely
filled with smoke. Tongues were well loosened
by then ; jest and banter flew round the younger
people, coarse enough at times, but always good-
humoured and taken in good part ; rough practical
jokes were played ; stories told, and riddles pro-
pounded ; while in one corner Robert discussed
serious matters with a few elders—the cost of food-
stuffs, or the price of pigs ; now and then raising his
voice in a vain appeal to " let people hear their
ears." At the back of the circle Hannah moved
about ceaselessly in a shallow pretence of housework,
rubbing this and polishing that, all the time keeping
up a stream of chaff and repartee, and playing off
one admirer nicely against another, with the cruelty
of the heartwhole. From such a bustling scene the
spirit-world seemed far distant. I forgot that the
longest evening will come to an end, and that,
sooner or later, I must go out into the dark.

But I would shortly be reminded of it.

About nine o'clock Robert went to bed. He was
a railway ganger, and had generally miles to walk

to his job. When he retired the elder members of the company went home. Robert's temper usually endured the increased noise about half an hour. Several times in that space his wife would be summoned " up the room," and would return with orders for "less noise"; but it was always quite clear from her manner that she sympathized with youthful high spirits, and I am afraid we paid little attention to her.

Finally came Robert's exasperated bellow, demanding to know " who the devil could go to sleep with that row going on." It was then that voices lowered, and chairs were drawn up to the fire, and ghost stories began.

Now was Mary's hour. Hitherto her gentle presence had been obscured by her sister's flaunting charms ; but now her mild influence flooded the room like moonlight, and subdued our souls to awe. Her pale, transparent features took on something of the mystic as she spoke ; we saw her fate in her face ; and listened to her as to one who was nearer the other world than we. It was not by Mary that my soul was filled with the terror by night. Her imagination rapt her above the grotesque and the horrible. The spirits that visited Mary had their habitation in the upper air.

But of the grotesque and the horrible we had plenty. The rest of the company leaned to the traditional, the clanking chain, the white sheet, hollow moans, and furniture that stirred without mortal agency. I became expert in the habits of ghosts, and skilled in divining omens. Magpies and rooks became birds of fate to me. The death-watch deferred my slumbers. In those days I had no mind to die sleeping. I knew that the solemn knocks portending death were always three in number. I have heard them sound many a night, and hoped they were for my uncle. I learned why ghosts " walked " ; and from the circumstances of a spirit's departure could nicely have estimated its chances of quiet rest. Any ghost, it is true, was liable to return, generally to a churchyard, though sometimes to the spot where it had quitted the body ; but in many cases the likelihood was greatly increased, and in some return was certain. The spirits of unchristened children, for example, always returned. But these were hardly numbered among my terrors. For some reason I saw them with my mind's eye as little blind kittens, and had pity for them, but no fear.

Deaths by violence or misadventure were fruitful of ghosts, suicides especially. These yielded a most unpleasant class of apparition, given to harrowing reproductions of the rash act that has cut them off from life. Murderers " walked "—that is, if they had been detected and duly hanged. A malevolent and dangerous class these (Robert Murray the younger was fond of relating a narrow escape he had from one of them), fortunately restricted to the neighbourhood of their crimes. Persons wrongfully dispossessed of houses or lands became a nightly burden to their dispossessors, but were seldom visible to anybody else, and might be set down as negligible. Buried money and hidden wills were accountable for another more or less harmless body of ghosts, too much occupied with their quest to concern themselves with the living, but troublesome, and in time apt to become wearing. Mrs. Murray had been pestered out of a comfortable house in her early days by such an absent-minded spirit, not to speak of twenty-five pounds she had lost through his forgetfulness while in the flesh.

All this grisly lore, and much besides, I received without question. I compiled a mental catalogue of all the troubled spirits that had walked our neighbourhood within living memory, and could have filled in an outline ghost-map of the district five miles round my uncle's house. Thereon I could have marked not only legitimate ghosts, of men and women once alive and dreading ghosts themselves, but banshees, black dogs, and will-o'-the-wisps; and fairy thorns, round which the little people danced each moonlight night, and might not be looked upon without deadly harm.

I have outgrown all these phantoms. I have enshrined reason, and am become material. No goblins haunt my night journeys. Darkness and light are alike untenanted for me. I could root up a fairy thorn nowadays, and fear no evil.

It is not all advantage. There is departed with

my childish bogies much that I would not willingly
have sacrificed. The fairies no longer dance in
the moonlight, yet now how gladly would my eyes
behold them. How gladly would I renew the terrors
of that walk from my Cousin Joseph's if the old man
were still there to hearten me on my way, and if
my feet were still bringing me home.

CONVERSATIONS LEXICON

THE library in our house was also the lumber room. All the rubbish of a generation had found its way there. The room was seldom entered by any adult member of the household except to add some fresh specimen to the collection. It was my kingdom. I had good times as a little boy, as good as any other country boy, and better than any town one; but the happiest hours of all I spent squatted on the dusty floor of the lumber-room poring over some dog-eared volume, often far above my childish under-standing. It was then I first tasted the pleasures of the imagination, and discovered that man could make out of his brain a brighter, more desirable world than this everyday earth; and could betake himself thither when the old world became too burdensome. I took too much of my exercise in that new world, and sowed the seeds of dyspepsia and short-sight thereby. But my bane brought its antidote with it. I learned to rank a good book above a good dinner; and if my sight is short, perhaps I can see more with it than some who have it longer.

When meals were ready I was always sought in

the lumber-room. And then, when the barn had been explored, and the stable, and the hayloft, and the garden, and the grove of trees beyond the paddock, I was sought there again. Only in my direst extremity of wrong-doing would some elder seek me in person. The steep flight of stairs, little better than a ladder, that led to my enchanted attic, was my protection. No one willingly toiled up that ascent. Not the maids, for they feared to discover work there. Not my aunt, for her shortness of breath. Not my uncle, for private reasons of his own. I lingered till wrath was as hot as dinner was cold, reading furiously in hope of reaching some duller passage before the menacing note that preluded an ascent should sound on my ears ; and, in the trance of some delightful paragraph, a new discovery or an old favourite, staving off the inevitable moment with a series of absent-minded assurances that I was " coming."

There have been no books written since like the ones I read then, and there never will be. Even they themselves are not the same. There is not the same savour in a tournament now as in the days when I was Ivanhoe, and overthrew Front-de-Bœuf with a lance made out of a withered hollyhock, and marred my Cousin Barbara's cheek for a twelve-month. Many a wonder has shrunk into the ordinary since then. Rupert Donnerhugel's two-handed brand has only one hilt now, and Christian's two-edged sword but a single blade. Brian de

Boys-Gilbert pronounces his name quite differently in these sophisticated days, and isn't the man he was ; and though the Sangreal is still a shadowy substance, it is no longer contained in my aunt's willow-pattern soup tureen.

It was in those days that I first knew the joys of battle—in Josephus' *Wars of the Jews*. I shared my discovery with the milk-cart driver, a bloody-minded youth like myself. He was a strong Orange-man, and as soon as he learned that the fighting was about religion he became as eager to listen as I was to read ; but when in course of time it emerged that the Pope as then was not, he couldn't see what there was to fight about, and left me to finish the book alone. In those days, too, I read Gibbon's *Decline and Fall*, in a one-volume edition printed in what I know now to be " Minion " type, and ruined my eyesight and my English style for ever.

My chiefest treasure was *Cassell's Penny Readings*, that admirable miscellany. Here first I met Kinglake, and the tall busby, and the thin red line. Scott's version of " The Wild Huntsman " was there, too. I remember the fearsome illustration. My mind was attuned to such horrors. That frenzied horseman with his hell-hounds swept the Barony of Lecale nightly for years after. Then there were the illustrations of Froissart's *Battle of Otterbourne*, with the moonlight glinting on the corsleted dead. I forgot my Scots blood in sympathy with the losing side, and have hardly yet got over my sorrow that Sir Henry Percy did not recover his pennon.

But a certain set of volumes stands out in my memory before all my other books. One of the minor tragedies of my childhood was connected therewith. It was an Encyclopædia in ten volumes. I recall them clearly, their grey dust-covers, and scarlet edges, and the bright blue cloth binding patterned in gold. The title was *The Popular Encyclopædia, or Conversation's Lexicon*. I missed the apostrophe in the sub-title, taking the word lexicon for an unknown adjective archaically placed after its noun, and found the phrase attractive, though I sometimes wondered how one carried on lexicon conversations. At first the books brought pleasure and interest into my life. The full-page plates I loved especially. About that time I was in search of a new career, having in turn given up piracy and soldiering; and the illustrations of steam-engines fixed my wandering fancy for a while. I remember, too, that from another plate I became acquainted with the interior wonders of the human frame; and abandoned the art of walking on my hands, just as I had nearly mastered it, from a feeling that it was better to let well alone.

The mass of information in the letterpress filled me with joy. I took all learning for my province, and hugged myself that there was so much to know, and that so few people could be aware of that. I used to cram up some out-of-the-way subject, and then artfully lead up to it in conversation, and made no small reputation in this way, particularly at school.

This display of knowledge was my undoing. Not content to shine merely among my fellows I must show off my learning before the Master himself. I did this partly out of vanity, but not altogether. There was policy in it, too. Many a time when my lessons were not too well learnt I belied the anticipative tingling of my palm by a timely display of supererogatory knowledge. At length the Master began to observe that the range of my information was beyond the ordinary, and sought the reason. I was but too glad to disclose it ; and not only told him of the *Popular Encyclopædia*, but in a folly compounded partly of pride, partly of sycophancy, offered to lend him the precious volumes. I had reckoned without my aunt. When I asked her permission she refused it flatly. She had lent books before, she said, and remembered what had happened to them. If the schoolmaster didn't know all he needed to know, at his time of life, it was a shame for him. Let him buy books if he wanted them. She had never heard the like. The next thing she supposed would be his wife would be asking her to tea.

My aunt was so very hot upon the subject that in any other circumstances I would have yielded silently.

But this was no ordinary case. I had volunteered the loan in humble propitiation, as some meek pagan might have vowed his choicest wether to the altar of Hades, and my offering had found favour. Not even the most superstitious of heathen could have quailed more at the prospect of drawing near the temple giftless than I did at the thought of going to school next day without the promised book. The Master had the reputation—with parents—of being a just man ; but the justice of the grown-up has to the young very much the appearance of tyranny, and we esteemed him harsh. To tell the truth, justice was the last thing I was seeking. Hitherto, from a social standing a little above the average in a country school, and a certain flashiness of parts, I had enjoyed a degree of favouritism, and had traded on it, and was loth to forfeit it. I was too well aware that an impartial report of my school-work would speedily lead to the curtailment of my dear, desultory readings, and I grieved at the thought of giving up Malory for Euclid. True, I might say my aunt had forbidden me to lend the books ; but danger lay that way also. I knew the Master's disconcerting intuition too well to hope that he would not perceive the implie dslight, and saw myself a vicarious sufferer for my aunt's snobbishness. I pleaded with her, but to little purpose. The utmost my entreaties could wring from her was that I might lend the Master an old two-volume edition of *Chambers's Encyclopædia*. I was to palm it off as the real Simon Pure. He would never know the difference, my aunt said. But I remembered too well my boasting of the ten beautiful blue-cloth volumes, and found no comfort in her words. Besides, my self-respect rebelled against the insincerity. I would rather have faced the penalties of direct refusal than have attempted that degrading subterfuge.

I spent a night of weeping and rebellious thought, and arose to crime. When I entered school that morning I laid the first volume of the *Conversations Lexicon* on the Master's desk, and along with it — a supplementary offering — the two-volume *Chambers's*. The ten dust-covers of the *Conversations* stood up erect and portly as before, but one of them, a little more portly than the others, but less fortified with learning, must have shared my tremblings when my aunt's footsteps approached that steep little stair.

My crime was not without recompense. I set home-lessons at naught while the Master was working through the *Conversations*, perfecting myself in Malory, and making further inroads on Gibbon. But I paid bitterly in the end. The shadow that had fallen between my aunt and me was not lifted when the Master had finished with the *Encyclopædia*. Just as my conscience began to feel a lightening, disaster befell me—at the ninth volume. On my coming home from school, I had hidden it in the cavity of the hollow ash, that I might restore it to its place in the bookcase after dark. When I returned it was gone. I remember how frantically I hunted through the little copse, sobbing and distraught, and returned every now and then to the hollow tree, insisting to my incredulous mind that it *must* be there. I dared not make inquiry among the servants. For weeks I wandered deviously about the garden and farmyard in an unhoping search. Gradually I desisted. In time the sense of disaster began to weigh less on me. But always at the back of my mind there remained a little canker of uneasiness. I used to lie awake at nights, and picture some lucky happening, such as a fire, that might wipe out the evidence of my crime for ever. I even thought of bringing about a small conflagration myself ; and if I could have been sure I would burn down nothing but the attic I think I would have risked it. Still more dreadful imaginings visited me. I saw myself assisting at the obsequies of my aunt, weeping, yet supported in my grief by the thought that now she could never know I had lost the ninth volume of the *Conversations Lexicon*. Then I would feel I was a very wicked little boy, and could scarcely wait for morning lest I myself should die before I had confessed my crime ; though I never did confess when morning came. But I laid up treasure against the day of discovery, becoming a better boy towards my aunt, less disobedient and neglectful, more eager to anticipate her wishes. This was the easier for me because I had left off my reading, and only stole up to the attic now and then to look inside the dust cover of the ninth volume in case a miracle should have happened. My health improved under this change of habits. It would have been better for me, for both worlds, if I had continued in my state of Damocles. But my deliverance was decreed.

One day as I was wandering restlessly about the house my aunt asked me a little sharply if I could find nothing to do but tramp up and down and destroy the carpets. What had come over me, she asked, that never used to have my nose out of a book. She did not wait for an answer, but clapped her hands suddenly, and rose and went into her bedroom. When she came back she bore in her hand a volume of the *Encyclopædia*. I was a very careless and forgetful little boy, she said, to leave a valuable book like that in the stump of a tree. It might have lain there till Doomsday if her bantam hen hadn't taken to laying away. But she was as bad as I was, she declared to her goodness, for she had forgotten hiding the book to give me a fright. I was to put it in its place, and promise never to take a book out of the house again, and she would say no more about it.

I did not need a second telling, as you may guess, but hurried up the stairs. As I sat on the ground before the complete ten volumes of the *Conversations Lexicon* I thought I should never be unhappy again. Then I remembered that my aunt did not know I had lent the books to the Master. In my exaltation I resolved to tell her, and clear my conscience altogether. But on reflection I decided to let sleeping dogs lie ; and sat down on the floor again with Gibbon, and finished the siege of Constantinople.

A POACHER

I WAS a poacher in my young days. An Englishman will think this disgraceful. To him a poacher is an evil-doer who does not respect the rights of property. But in the County Down of my childhood we had very democratic notions about game birds, and did not recognize private ownership of them at all. A poacher to us was simply a person who brought himself under the law by carrying a gun without Government licence ; and even in the North-East corner of our island no one is looked down on for breaking a law he does not like. One or two farmers, who aspired to the Commission of the Peace, or lived near a police-barracks, took out ten-shilling licences " to carry and use a gun "; and " the gentry " were understood to pay incredible sums for the privilege of shooting game ; but the percentage of guns that contributed to the upkeep of Her Majesty's Government—I write of Victorian days—was small. Our local landowners made little attempt to preserve game ; yet there were few districts where it would more have needed preservation. There was scarcely a kitchen fireplace in the Barony of Lecale but some old fowling-piece hung on a couple of nails above it.

We had no neat hammerless guns in those days, to make killing easy. Even double-barrels were rare, and conferred dignity on their possessors. On Saint Stephen's Day, when old and young went forth to kill, I have seen converted Brown Besses do their part ; huge engines of destruction, with a barrel as long as a fishing-rod and as wide as a gutter-pipe ; historic relics that might in their time have hurled defiance and an ounce and a half of lead against the French at Salamanca or Waterloo.

In those days smokeless cartridges were not. Dense fumes of sulphur filled the sportsman's eyes after his shot, and prolonged the hopes of the unskilful. There were, indeed, no cartridges. We loaded by the muzzle, then. It was an empirical business with most of us. The timid and the finicky might nicely estimate their charge with powder-horn and shot-bag, but the impecunious, which embraced all small boys, measured with the open palm and put their trust in a tough barrel and a strong collar-bone.

First went in your powder, then a wad of news-paper—we called this " colfin," I remember—on which you hammered till your ramrod would leap clean out of the barrel ; then your shot, or " hail," and another wad of " colfin," the last not too tightly hammered if you valued your shoulder. Before placing your cap it was well to look in the nipple for the glittering grains of black powder. Without this precaution miss-fires took place ; and apart from the frustration of your deadly purpose, miss-fires were undesirable. When the cap snapped and no explosion followed you did well, if you were a little boy, to lay your gun on the ground and withdraw to the rear, lest after some inward meditation it should decide to go off after all. I had an action of battery against a gun-butt many a time before I fathomed the mysteries of priming and the deceitfulness of damp powder.

I began my shooting career with a humbler weapon than a gun. I was my own gunsmith, and my fire-arm a pistol made of elderwood, or as we call it, " boortree." But my quarry, though I did not know it, was noble, being no less than a little boy of nine. I only just failed to bag him. The greater portion of my pistol returned to its original elements on the occasion ; the rest is still embedded in my right thumb. So I never killed anything with my boortree pistol, thereby falsifying much prophecy. But the disaster to my thumb more than satisfied my aunt's ambitions as a Cassandra ; and lest a worse thing should befall I was by her good offices with my uncle promoted to a single-barrelled snipe-gun that had been my grandfather's, and took the field in earnest.

It was one thing to possess a gun and another to find a mark for it. The harvest was scarce on account of the multitude of labourers. Nothing that flew or ran wild lived long in the County Down of my childhood, if only it was eatable. If a covey of partridges ever flew into our district from a far-off demesne I am persuaded it never alighted. As for hares, the rumour of one mobilized every gun for five miles round. The L—— hounds were called harriers ; but it was a courtesy title. If a single dog of the pack could have distinguished between the scent of a hare and of a red-herring the knowledge came through heredity and not experience.

Yet one famous hare sojourned on Hazel Knowe Hill a whole winter, defying fate and powder ; a thing incredible had the fact not been attested by numbers of the unsuccessful, who swore to her tattered ear. In time she became legendary. Dick Murray saw her once, and said she was as big as a calf. According to some she had the power of being in two places at the same time. Others said she was a witch and could only be killed by a silver bullet. The L—— harriers drew Hazel Knowe Hill three times for her in vain ; after which a generation of sceptics arose who denied her existence.

But such a hare there was, for I beheld her miserable end at the hands of Robert Seeds, the roadman, the meanest pot-hunter that ever drew trigger, a man never known to burn powder on anything flying, or even running. Stalking this murderer one evening at a distance of a hundred yards or so in hope of the reversion of something he should miss, I saw him suddenly point his gun at a tussock of long grass almost at his feet and fire both barrels. I ran up to find him ruefully gazing at the limbs of the famous hare. The body he had blown to fragments. The tattered ear was there, however, plain to be recognized, and might have made the foundation of a fairer fame for Robert ; for wanting a witness to the deed no one would have believed the great hare could have fallen ignominious, a sitting shot. But I refused Robert's proffered fourpence, and what was harder to refuse, a single-bladed sailor's knife, the very thing for a young pirate, and took good care that on one occasion at least murder did out.

Such quarry as partridges or hares seldom fell my way. Wood pigeon, or green plover, with an occasional rabbit, stood at the top of my bill of fare. I say of my bill of fare, for it was a point of duty with me to eat all I slew. For this reason after my first year's shooting I spared water-hens. True, a water-hen may be eaten, and is certainly better-flavoured than a coot ; but when one has said this the limits of eulogy have been reached. To sportsmen of above twelve years of age I do not recommend either bird. But the small fowler should not too early despise the day of blackbirds. They are toothsome little fowl, and if you are pleased to imagine yourself Lemuel Gulliver, make quite respectable capons ; though it will occur to you that Lemuel must have very often gone hungry to bed on his first voyage.

Perhaps I should have done better to shoot as well as eat in the country of imagination. There are no ten-shilling licences in shadowland. When

I went forth as Uncas or Hawk-Eye, and my flintlock was an ash sapling, and I tracked the noble savage through the pathless forests of my uncle's planting, though my bag was lighter my mind was more at ease. The actual practice of shooting was a wearing business. There were jealous landowners to be looked out for, and cranky farmers, and the police, and an elusive and sinister being known as " the gauger," who spent his days searching for the unlicensed, and had power to mulct in fearful penalties. When you saw such a one in the distance —and to the uneasy conscience he was Protean in his shapes—you hid your gun among the briers and looked cherubic and picked blackberries. Only, if you were prudent, you thrust your gun into the briers muzzle foremost, so that when pulling it out again you avoided receiving the charge in your diaphragm, a catastrophe I nearly failed to avoid once—by inches. That and a certain tame goose I once shot are among the humiliations of my sporting career. Still, Time brought in his revenges. Years afterwards I served up that goose, with brier trimmings, to a kindly editor, and recovered my seven-and-sixpence with large interest. But I still blush over two pickles of lead in old Tom Brogan's ankle. He showed me them while he and I were hunting for the miscreant who had fired the shot, a tall, dark man with a beard, as I described him, who was never again seen in the country. I shiver yet when I remember how narrowly we escaped finding his gun.   It was a light single-barrel, and had once belonged to his grandfather.

I should have been more careful with a gun. I had been well schooled to prudence, and by the best shot and the keenest sportsman I have ever known.   This was my Uncle Bob, who was not my uncle at all, or any relation, but an old family friend whom I had adopted to uncleship.   Privately, between myself and my imagination, he was really Rip Van Winkle.   And indeed, as I remember him, he might have come straight down from the Kaatskill Mountains after awakening from his long sleep. I am sure my Uncle Bob's beard was as long and straggly as Rip Van Winkle's, and had been innocent of a barber for quite as many years ; and his shooting-coat was quite as old, and his complexion as weathered with sun and frost and rain.   But though it is probable that Rip Van Winkle's eyebrows had grown grey and bushy like my uncle's, the eyes that looked out under them could never have been so keen and piercing ; and I am certain that Rip Van Winkle was not so good a shot.   Lastly, I know very well that no woman in the Kaatskill or the parts round about could have henpecked my Uncle Bob.

He lived some miles away, in a country of bog and woodland, where game would have been more plentiful than with us if my Uncle Bob had not lived there.   By profession he was a farmer, but shooting was his calling.   All his energies were directed to the destruction of wild life.   In antediluvian days he

would have been as great a hunter as Nimrod
himself, perhaps a greater. When Nimrod was a
boy of seventy or so I cannot think he knew as
much of the habits of game as my uncle did, or had
killed as many hares and pheasants and partridges
and wild ducks, or was as anxious to kill more. I
would have backed my Uncle Bob against him any
day at finding a hare, or divining where a covey of
partridges would alight, or at what freshet you had
best wait for wild-duck on a frosty evening.

I do not know whether you could have said that
my Uncle Bob loved wild birds and animals, yet his
passionate preoccupation had something of the
quality of love. And he was merciful towards them
according to his lights, and would have followed a
wounded partridge half-a-day that he might put it
out of its misery.

It is hard to think how he ever came to reach
seventy years of age. He was a frail man to look at,
and took little account of health when game birds
were in question. Walking with him across his
fields or among the cattle in his farmstead you would
behold an absent-minded old man, with restless,
wandering hands and a head a little shaken with
palsy. Very likely he would be talking to himself,
and not heeding what you said to him, especially if
you spoke of farming. But place a gun in his hands,
and flush a covey out of the turnips, and you would
see a figure of whipcord and steel and a gun that
had become part of it ; and when the gun came

down from his shoulder there would be birds to retrieve.

If you had been trained under my Uncle Bob you would never have dragged a gun after you through a hedge, or brought one loaded into a house, or levelled it at anyone even when it was empty, or aimed at a blackbird when old Tom Brogan stood directly in the line of fire ; or if you had been a little dreamer, as I was, and done any of these things, your calves and the ramrod of a gun would have become acquainted.

My Uncle Bob never had a miss-fire in all his life, or frightened a horse by firing too near the county-road, or killed or injured a man, or shot a ferret. And he left behind him disciples scarcely less careful than himself.

He is buried in a little, lonely churchyard by the side of a moorland bog. There is no other tenant. The churchyard was consecrated specially that he might be laid in that spot. It was thought a happy choice for the resting-place of the old fowler. But above his head on a winter's night sounds the plaintive note of the curlew, and the drumming of the snipe ; and I wonder that he lies so quiet there. They should have laid his gun by his side, that when he rises in the flesh he might have one last shot before he goes to his account for the beautiful wild creatures that he knew and understood, and, after his nature, killed.

THE GATE OF HORN

IN the good old times when magicians were not confined to story books but visibly walked the earth, a necromancer beginning his incantations always cast a handful of aromatic herbs into his brazier. I used often to wonder why this was. I know now there are a number of quite learned explanations of the rite ; but I have never read any of them. I practised necromancy a good deal in my childhood, raiding my aunt's cupboard, to her frequent mystification, for any likely substance from green tea to flowers of sulphur ; but never succeeded in evoking any spirits, probably because I was secretly very much afraid I might succeed. But perhaps the real reason was that I was too young. When you come to think of it, all the eminent necromancers were elderly men. I believe if one is old enough, one can summon forth the spirits of departed men and women without any fumigation at all. Nevertheless fumigation is a help. I know that now, for by its aid I have just performed my first successful experiment in necromancy, though quite unintentionally. Going through the pockets of a little boy of my acquaintance to-night after he had departed to bed I came on a fragment of horn, and thinking there was quite enough rubbish in the little boy's pocket without that and several other small matters. I laid it aside. The other trifles, of rusty nails and such-like, I presently threw out, but the fragment of horn I dropped into the fire. I muttered no incantation; but I must now be past the age when incantations are necessary, for no sooner had the heavy, sickly smell struck on my nostrils than looking through the dim smoke I saw old William McCoubray, the blacksmith. The off hind-hoof of my uncle's bay horse, Johnny, was resting on his leather apron; the old man picked up a hot shoe with his pincers and pressed it to the hoof; the dun smoke rose in clouds from the sizzling horn; he wryed his head aside and blew the smoke towards me; the heavy, sickly smell struck on my nostrils; and I myself was a little boy again.

There is no more attractive place for a little boy than a blacksmith's shop, and surely no kindlier blacksmith than William McCoubray ever presided over one. He was a long, thin figure of a man, not a bit like the traditional blacksmith, and his face was long and thin too, and of a rather melancholy expression, tending more to resignation than to repining. It was his habit every now and then, when he thought himself unobserved, to pause in his work, and shaking his head slowly up and down, to sigh forth his plaintive murmur against life: " Ay, ay—dear ay."

I am not sure that William found blacksmithing a very lucrative calling ; but his melancholy did not spring from that, but was connected with a little blacksmith who had come into the world many years before, and left it again before he had learned even the trade of living. It was a pity ; for beyond doubt he would have been a great blacksmith. William often told me of him when he and I were alone, of his sturdy arms and legs and the deep chest of him— " not like my pigeon-breast," William would say— and how strongly he could grip his father's fore-finger, just as if he was laying hold of the handle of the big " sledge." He was the only little blacksmith that had been vouchsafed to William and his wife, and William thought he left the world before his father got any good of him. But William was wrong. He made a big corner in his father's heart for a long succession of little boys to creep into. It was for his sake, though I didn't know it then, that I was allowed to range William's forge at will, and upset his nail-box, and blunt his whittle, and mislay his rasp and his pincers, and even break a " sledge " handle now and then, unreproved.

I have in my memory a rich store of sights and sounds and smells that I laid up in William's forge ; the dazzling, quivering glow of incandescent metal as it was drawn from the fire ; the intense white radiance of the fire itself when the bellows were in full blast, and the blue flame that played over it when the bellows were at rest—which was not often when I was in the shop; the flat sheets of sparks that flew beneath each stroke of the great sledges; the clank and wheeze of the bellows and the roar of the fierce flame; the upthrown head and clattering hoofs of a startled horse; the restless pawing of an impatient one; the alternate thud and ringing clink as William struck the softened metal and his anvil time about, for some occult reason known to blacksmiths only, though I was always careful to follow his practice myself when he allowed me to spoil a shoe now and then; the short, sharp hiss as he plunged a finished shoe into the cooling-trough; the inky water in the trough, from which, for some odd reason, I first formed a visual image of the River Styx; the light fragments of iron leaf that floated thereon, and the thin steam that wandered over its surface; the smell of burnt hoof and singed apron; the thick smoke that hung above our heads and stole away little by little through the open door; all these came back to me in the fumes of my piece of horn.

During the years that I lived with my uncle he had the best-shod horses in County Down. I saw to that. No ear about the farm was so keen to detect the clank of a loosened shoe as mine, and no eye so sharp to observe a worn one. Our horses never came to disaster of broken knees on the ice-bound roads. At the first frosty twinkle of a star I was importuning our head ploughman to have his team "sharped." Riding horses to the forge was

my perquisite.   Bareback I ranged the wide pampas
that stretched along the road between our house
and William McCoubray's, out-galloped the fierce
Apache, and hunted down the buffalo and the casso-
wary.   I have encountered the Soldan Saladin many
a time on that journey, and overthrown Conrade of
Montserrat more than once.   The mark is just
becoming visible with my receding hair, relic of the
day when the Master of the Knights Templar
withstood me in the shape of an elm tree, and I
vanished unknightly over the tail through my lance's
refusal to splinter.   William McCoubray little knew
how often Ivanhoe, or the Black Knight, or Don
Quixote has clattered up to his forge-door, and
thrown his reins to a fair page, and quaffed a beaker
—sometimes of butter-milk—at the hands of that
high-born maiden his daughter Martha.

If I dropped out of romance into reality when I
entered William's shop, it was no less enthralling.
The stages from the bar of iron to the finished shoe
were a procession of delights to a little boy, and only
less attractive the operations of fitting the shoe and
nailing it on the hoof.   Then there were old shoes
to be sorted out, and new ones to be cooled, and the
bellows to be blown, and nails to be straightened on
the old anvil in the corner.   There were no neat
boxes of shining nails to be had from the iron-
monger in those days.   Each blacksmith made his
own nails.   I have often seen the bundles of long
nail rods being delivered at William's shop, tied in

the middle with straw rope, and clashing frantically with every jolt of the cart as they came up to the door. When Jove brandished his thunderbolts in the course of my reading it was always a bundle of red-hot nail-rods he grasped in his hand. I sometimes made a few nails myself when there was a stray end of nail-rod to be had ; but I have never seen mine used. William explained to me that the nails I made could be used only for a donkey's shoes, and no donkey ever happened to come to the forge while I was there.

There were quite a number of interesting things about nails. For example, nails withdrawn from an old shoe and no longer fit for use were called " horse-stumps." They acquired an unusual toughness by wear. Gun-barrels were made from them. A gun-barrel made from horse-stumps could not burst. I know this is true ; for I tried the effect of a treble charge on a single-barrelled gun of my uncle's reputed to be made of horse-stumps, and only succeeded in blowing out the nipple.

I never quite believed in the horse-stump legend till I tried this experiment ; for it was from Hughey Dixon, William's assistant, I had learned it ; and Hughey was so notorious a wag, or in our speech, " sconce," that even I didn't believe all he said. He was a huge man, flabby for a blacksmith, with a broad face that sweated continually. He worked hard, but laughed harder, and so grew fat. I disliked him in the daytime ; for in daytime there were seldom sufficient objects for his unending chaff to divert it from me. He clouded the pleasure of my visits to the forge for quite a long time by inventing an intrigue between myself and an elderly maiden lady who owned a neighbouring farm, and had once or twice given me bread and sugar on my way to William McCoubray's. There was never anything between Miss McKelvey and me but this matter of bread and sugar; but I was unwise in protesting that so violently to Hughey; and he caused me a good deal of pain by affecting to disbelieve me. Gossip strongly affirmed that Miss McKelvey was in the habit of praying for a man. If she had but known it, at one time her petition was nightly supported in the orisons of a certain little boy.

I lived the scandal down in time, though Providence did not intervene on my behalf—or Miss McKelvey's; and the full pleasure of my daylight visits to the forge returned. But the long nights of the ploughing season were still the greater joy. It was then that ploughmen came to William's to have their plough-socks pointed. The sock of a plough is the portion of it that enters the ground first, and consequently wears away most speedily. It is detachable from the plough-frame, so that it may be re-pointed, which in ploughing time becomes necessary every few days. When I was a boy the ploughmen tramped to the forge and back after hours. Later they began to object to this, and insisted on stopping work in time for the journey to be performed before instead of after supper-time. It is from this period that the farmer dates the spread of Socialism to the country districts. Nowadays, sock-points can be bought at a hardware shop so cheaply that they are not worth re-pointing, and the ploughman goes no more to the forge with them. Some of the brightness has gone out of his life thereby.

I remember those nights in William's forge; the circle of grinning ploughmen squatted on everything that could be turned into a seat, and, when the fire was blown up, the revelation of another tier of humanity on points of vantage round the walls; the clatter of jokes; the bantering of amateur hammermen as they strove to emulate Hughey's mighty strokes; the increasing triumphant roar of early-comers as each fresh ploughman appeared blinking in the doorway and laid his sock at the end of the long line on the ground. Dominant over clamour of tongues, and clang of hammers, and roar of fire, rang Hughey's mighty bellow as some shaft of his wit struck home. Woe betide the unhappy wight who should be detected trying to push his sock in, out of turn. His past was unrolled incident by incident before the delighted throng; and the commentary was worse than the text. The case of lovers was hardly more enviable. Many a love-lorn ploughman walked four additional miles to Johnny Dougherty's forge sooner than face Hughey's

tongue. And I, little sycophant, when a victim
offered, sat well within the circle of light that Hughey
might see, and laughed as loud as any.

It was generally in the company of our second
ploughman, Dick Murray—Slippery Dick, he was
nicknamed—that I visited the forge at night. Dick
was a wit-brother of Hughey's, with a twist of dry
humour in his composition that Hughey lacked.
The laughter that followed his sallies was as hearty,
but more good-natured. He knocked his man
down just as effectually as Hughey did ; but then in
some subtle way he picked him up again and dusted
him. A certain half-ironical tenderness tinged his
mockery of lovers ; for Dick was a great lover
himself. It was in consequence of this weakness of
his that I kept so good hours on the nights I visited
the forge.

But though I always quitted the scene unsatiated
I never failed to enjoy the little comedy that preceded
our departure. Dick always sat beside the forge-fire,
and though the others did not know, his sock lay
under the skirts of his coat with a large plug of
tobacco concealed in the hollow of it. When a
particular significant cough of Dick's showed that
time pressed I knew what would happen. Hughey
would lay down on the forge the sock he was working
on at the moment and grope among the cinders for
his pipe. To all seeming he resumed his interrupted
task. But I knew that when that sock was finished
it would turn out to be Dick Murray's, and made my

way to the door. There I waited with suppressed glee Hughey's start of surprise and discovery, and Dick's protestations ; and as the pair of us fled down the road pursued by a volley of contumely, I felt that I partook vicariously in Dick's glory, and thought we were two very clever fellows.

But I always yearned after the joys from which I was untimely banished, and one night visited the forge alone, and lingered to the end. I had done better to quit it while the tide of life ran strong. . . .

The smoke of my incantation is waning ; the fire sinks on the forge ; weariness falls even on Hughey's giant frame ; the laughter fails little by little ; one after another the ploughmen go out quietly into the night. Hughey himself is gone at last, and William McCoubray and I are left alone. I feel the kindly farewell pressure of his hand on my shoulder as he turns back into the dreary shop, and hear his patient soliloquy : " Ay, ay—dear ay."

A PLOUGHMAN'S COURTSHIP

I

PLOUGHING is no longer the skilled occupation it used to be. The modern chill-plough demands neither knowledge nor strength. Its guiding wheel measures off the furrow with a monotonous accuracy, and controls the depth of it to a fraction of an inch. Your chill-ploughed field is a depressing prospect of mechanical regularity. The personal touch is wanting. You may drive through County Down the whole of a Spring day and think the same ploughman has turned over every furrow you see. It was different in the days of the old swing-plough. Then a man could mark his individuality as clearly with the plough as with the pen. There was character in ploughing. The expert could recognize at a glance the style of any ploughman in his neighbourhood. Of any acknowledged craftsman that is ; the undistinguished mass of botchers merely turned over the earth ; they could not be said to plough. But the style of the masters was unmistakable. The respective furrows of Tom Lennon and William Brown were no more to be confounded than is the blank verse of Shakespeare with that of Milton.

Tom Lennons and William Browns there may still be among us, potential ploughmen great even as their fathers ; but their gift will never be revealed to them. A mechanical age has deprived them of their birthright. They are doomed to an accomplishment of flat mediocrity, and will go down to the grave without their meed of fame.

It is true that ease has come to man and horse. The poet can no longer write of the " swinkt ploughman " ; " steaming " is no longer the fit adjective for his yoke. The straining horses no longer vivify the landscape with energy embodied ; they have sunk to mere prettiness as they amble across lea or stubble, scarce heeding the trivial machine behind. Then, to guide the old swing-plough was a strong man's job. Every faculty was at strain during the arduous voyage from hedge to hedge. The instinctive eye might measure the due line, but every trick of horse-craft, every effort of muscle, was needed to counteract the hundred influences that contended against a straight furrow. Nor was the struggle conducted in silence. From the moment when his sock-point entered the soil until he emerged sweating on the opposite head-rig the ploughman's voice never failed in a stream of admonishment, reproof, or encouragement to his striving team. " Get along, Johnny, get along with you—steady, Dobbin, steady ! —good horses, good horses "—mingled with the technical ejaculations : " Hup, hup—wind, wind," as the team turned towards the furrow or away from it ; and all the time the ploughman's earth-clogged feet sought purchase on the uneven ground, and his hands gripped tense on the shafts of his rocking plough. It cannot be denied that ease has come to the ploughman, also. But while to his horses the change is perhaps all gain, the ploughman himself has paid a heavy price for it. He has lost interest in his calling since it was degraded to the mere mechanical. He no longer discusses his craft with his fellow-artists at a four-roads or over a cottage fire, or walks five miles of a Sunday, as I have known William Brown do, to view and criticize the accomplishment of a rival. No man is proud of his ploughing nowadays, or envies another's.

There is worse to come. One glory at least has survived the coming of the chill-plough, the birds. The long line of rooks still stretches from the plough-man's heels, as if he were ploughing birds out of the earth ; the scolding seagulls still hover above the new-made furrow, a dazzle of beating wings. I loved the Spring ploughing, and " mitched " from school many a Spring day to follow the plough. I saw my Mother Earth in the rich brown tilth as never in other aspects. In Autumn, I forgot the giver in the plenteousness of the gift. Then, too, I loved the great cotton-wool clouds, a little soiled on the under-surface in the early weeks, but bleaching to white purity as the season advanced ; I loved the gleam of sunlight on wet tree-bole in the bordering copse ; and rejoiced to mark the cold grey field-pools warm to azure. But most of all I loved the following birds whose tireless energy of beak and wing mocked man's sedater bread-winning. I delighted in the clamour of their unending squabble for existence, the petulant scream of the seagull, the deeper expostulation of the rook, the jostlings for some fat worm, the preoccupied leap-frog, half vault, half flutter, as each bird strove to approach nearer to the ploughman's heels. My eye joyed in the metallic iridescence of blues and greens on a rook's back as he stalked from furrow to furrow with an embarrassed gravity, as if a Bishop should walk on stilts ; or the delicate poise of an alighting gull, with upstretched fluttering wings and tentative feet. I lay aside my brief against the chill-plough. We are threatened by a greater evil. The motor tractor is at our gates, noisy and noisome, and the ploughman's birds will soon follow him no more.

I mean well by William Brown when I hope he has been delivered from the evil of tractors to come. And if he has passed to a happier world, killed as I have little doubt by the chill-plough, I trust that, in another sense of the word, there is husbandry in Heaven. For William was a ploughman incarnate. Every impulse of his soul strove towards perfection in his craft ; all else was trivial to him. As truly as he ploughed to live he lived but to plough. He used to say he would wish to die between the shafts ; but surely not that he might be transported to some region of ploughless bliss.

It is no sarcasm to say that William did my uncle the honour of becoming his first ploughman for several years ; for it was in William's power to confer honour on his master. The fame of his ploughing spread over two baronies. At ploughing-matches he towered above farmers of a hundred acres and more. I used to trot at his heels at these festivals, partaker of his glory, and drink in the respectful asides of bystanders that " there was William Brown, Mr. W——'s man." Our sideboard glittered with cups of William's winning ; for in those feudal days the master reaped where the man had sown. Legends sprang up about his ploughing. He could juggle with his plough, men averred. The topmost ridge of his furrow—the " combing," as it was technically known—was said to be so sharp that it cut the feet of alighting birds ; and I am willing to believe it, though I cannot say I ever observed the phenomenon myself.

It is sad to think that such a ploughman should have died and left the world no copy ; yet so it was. It has been the fate of the great artist in all ages : the one master passion occupies his soul to the exclusion of lesser affections : he must plough his lonely furrow. Perhaps it is better thus. No son of William's could have driven a motor tractor gladly.

II

Yet love knocked at William's heart once, and gained a partial entrance. Our servant-maid, Kate Keenan, wrought the mischief; a tall slip of a girl, scarce twenty, with dancing dark eyes, and a mass of purple-black hair always threatening to tumble down her back. There was a wild strain in Kate. She worked singing, idling by starts, then swooping at her task with a whirlwind rush that accomplished wonders in a marvellously short time, but was very severe on delf. She was given to cheap finery, and became the prey of every pedlar that unrolled his wares in our kitchen. In the most pressing necessity of stockings she would lay out her last coin on a showy hat. I have known her buy a diamond brooch—pedlar's diamonds—and blacklead her heels till the next monthly wages became due. And she was the only girl I ever saw play the Jew's Harp. Why stolid William Brown should become the sport of such a Venus it is hard to say; but before she had been with us a fortnight it was observed that he was lingering portentously over his evening porridge, and that his subsequent pipe was smoked by the kitchen fire instead of in the stable. He was never known to say anything to Kate during these sittings, and his intentions were in doubt for some weeks, till one evening he suddenly asked her if she would step as far as the top of the Whinny Hill with him before bed-time. There was great excitement in the farmstead over this unexpected move of William's. The progress of the pair was watched by half-a-dozen pairs of eyes from various places of concealment, my aunt, to preserve her dignity, peering out of an upstairs bedroom window. I had become fairly skilled in such matters by this time of my life, and was a good deal disappointed to perceive on Kate's return that her hair was no more disordered than usual, which I thought a bad sign. I was not sufficiently intimate with Kate to question her on the subject ; for she was a kindly soul, very fond of children, and prone to gusts of affection involving hugs and kissing, which caused me to hold her more aloof than any of our other maids. But my aunt could not contain her curiosity, and asked Kate if William had said anything. Kate told her he had not said anything either going or coming, but that passing through the haggard on their way back he had tried to put his arm round her, and she didn't permit him, because she thought there should be some conversation first. But William walked to the top of Whinny Hill with Kate several times during the following week, and towards the end of the week had found his tongue a little, it would seem, for our yard boy lay behind a hedge as they passed one evening, and heard him tell Kate that he had money saved. After this report got about, as the yard boy took very good care it should, it was taken for granted about the farm that William and Kate would shortly be married.

I think it might have come to marrying between them; for William was a personable man, tall, fair-haired, and ruddy-cheeked; and though he was staid beyond his years, he was a good-natured, likeable fellow. Then Kate was flattered by his attentions. He was a rising man. Already he received five pounds a year more than any plough-man in the district, and it was known that he was well into his second hundred of savings towards buying a farm. Besides, he had never been known to pay court to anyone before, and that in itself was a feather in Kate's cap.

I wasn't quite satisfied on William's account. I admired him and looked up to him as to a man gifted above ordinary ploughmen; and I was by no means sure that he wasn't being taken in.

I liked Kate very well; but she was too young and flighty for my taste, which at that time ran to the sober and mature among women-kind; and I felt that if William knew as much about her as I did he would very likely be of my opinion. I could see quite plainly he knew little about the real Kate, who was always very demure when he was in the kitchen; and thought at times it was my duty to enlighten him. In particular it was on my conscience that he should be told about the Jew's Harp. But when I hinted my scruples to my aunt she was greatly disturbed, and told me that I must never interfere between lovers. It was a very wicked thing to do, she said, and no good ever came of it.

I had never seen my aunt so moved before. All the same, she added, she would believe in the wedding when she saw it.

But William the ploughman stood greatly in the way of William the lover, and in the end proved the undoing of him altogether. It came about in this manner : Like all good ploughmen, William was much attached to his horses, and took great pride in their appearance. No better groomed or glossier pair than William's ever stepped before a plough. Their meals and toilet were his charge alone. He would allow no meaner hand to minister to them. Above all his charges he was attached to our bay mare, Betty. She was worthy of his love ; a handsome, docile creature, light for a plough-horse, but of a great heart. I have heard William say in an unwonted outburst of feeling that if he had Betty in the lead he could plough with a Newfoundland dog in the furrow. Nearly all his spare time went to burnishing her beautiful coat—a great deal more of it, indeed, than Kate approved of. I have seen Kate many a night stalking up and down the yard, stormy-faced, while William lingered in the stable to bestow a supererogatory touch of the currycomb on her rival.

But William went his preoccupied way unconscious of her rising indignation. The great Spring ploughing-match was at hand. His name was inscribed twice in succession on the H—— cup ; and three successive victories won it outright. That ploughing-match was to be William's Philippi had he but known it. Yet fate did her best for him; or perhaps it was the humbler divinity of Commonsense. He invited Kate to accompany him on the field, and partake of the triumph of which none of us stood in any doubt. Such a joint expedition was tantamount to a public betrothal. Every grievance vanished from Kate's volatile mind at the prospect of parading her new dignity before the notables of the country-side. In a nightly canvass of her finery she forgot William nearly as completely as William in his dream of fame forgot her.

To crown all her good-fortune a pedlar visited our house on the eve of the great day. I remember Kate's sparkling eyes and flushed cheeks as she tried on one gee-gaw after another, a Marguerite of the kitchen. My aunt caught the infection in the end, and became nearly as excited as Kate. I think we all went a little mad that night. I know my aunt allowed Kate to mortgage two full months' wages; and I, infected with Kate's recklessness, broke open my money-box, and bought myself a four-bladed knife.

Only one treasure remained for Kate to covet, a matter of half-a-dozen yards of lilac ribbon, discovered when she had sunk far below bankruptcy. In vain Kate tried the effect of it in her hair, and on her bosom, and against her neck, in vain the pedlar dangled it. My aunt hardened her heart, not indeed before it was time; and the lilac ribbon disappeared into the pack again. When the pedlar had gone we spread all the new finery on the kitchen table, and began to turn it over half-heartedly. There was something wanting, and we all knew it. We had sold the spirit of delight for half-a-dozen yards of lilac ribbon. Presently Kate bundled up her purchases and went off with them to her room. There was something disconsolate in her air. My aunt stood looking after her a moment, then drew out her purse and handed me half-a-crown, remarking acidly that she was an old fool. I needed no further hint, but took to my heels. When I reached our farmyard gate, to my surprise the pedlar was just passing out through it. I told him I wished to buy the lilac ribbon. He answered that he was sorry, but he had sold it to one of the men-servants. When I questioned him I found it was to William Brown, and ran hastily back to the kitchen with the news. My aunt and Kate looked at each other for a moment. " Oh, mem," said Kate ; that was all ; but I wish William could have heard her. My aunt declared to her goodness she didn't think William had it in him, and straightway hunted me off to bed.

I was very much disappointed and chagrined, and fought off sleep till my aunt's footsteps sounded on the stair. But when I asked her if William had brought the ribbon to Kate she gave me no satisfaction, demanding quite sharply why I wasn't asleep hours ago ; from which I concluded that he had not yet given Kate the ribbon. I had a dismal certainty that I should sleep late the next morning and miss the giving of the ribbon; and I knew from old experience that on a morning of any special activity no one would awaken me, so that I should be out of the way. And of course I did sleep late, so late that when I arrived downstairs it was almost time for William and Kate to start for the ploughing match. Kate was dressed ready to go out; but when I looked for the ribbon it was nowhere to be seen, and when I began to question my aunt about it she was even shorter with me that the night before.

Nine o'clock struck, the hour at which William and Kate were to leave; and there was no word of the ribbon. By this time Kate was half-crying, half-furious, and my aunt's attitude towards an inquisitive little boy was fairly insufferable. At last a knock came to the kitchen door. It was only the yard boy to say William was ready. "You may go, Kate," said my aunt, declaring bitterly to her goodness and patience that men were bigger fools than she thought. Neither she nor I followed Kate out of the kitchen.

It scarcely seemed a moment till the door opened again, and Kate flung in, scarlet-faced and sobbing. She did not answer my aunt's startled inquiry, but began to take off her hat. I could see that her hands were trembling. All at once she flopped down on a chair, and laughed and laughed. "Oh, mem," she said, "go and look!"

My aunt and I ran out. William Brown was

standing between the handles of his plough, looking back towards the kitchen door in bewilderment. My gaze travelled to his team. The bay mare's mane and tail were neatly plaited with lilac ribbon.

.   .   .   .   .   .

Kate married Dick Murray, a former second ploughman of ours, who took service again in our neighbourhood about then.   I was reminded of this story by looking at the H——— Cup not long ago, and seeing William Brown's name inscribed on it three years in succession.

PIGS

I NEVER became really friendly with a pig. Pigs collectively I liked, just as I liked hens and geese and sheep ; but I never singled out any individual as a special object of affection, as I have sometimes done with all the other species of animals on my uncle's farm. I never knew a pig by name. Yet pigs rightly considered are attractive animals. Common report deals hardly with them. To say that a man is as dirty as a pig is to insult the pig. For a pig is a clean animal when his master will permit him to be so. He does not dwell in his moist insanitary piggery from choice, but loves sweet, dry straw, and spends much of his time perambulating the dunghill to which he is condemned, in search of such a bed. We misapprehend his efforts to attain personal purity, and hold him up to obloquy where we should rather approve. The sow that returned to her wallowings in the mire was really seeking cleanliness. A fallible being will fail somewhere, Doctor Johnson has pithily said. The sacred writer, inspired only about heavenly things, in the matter of pigs was little better than one of the foolish.

Nor have profane writers dealt more happily with them. There was an old copy of the *Essays of Elia* in our lumber-room, when I was a boy. Even then I was a devoted Elian, but I could never quite forgive Lamb for his callous attitude towards sucking pigs. His heartless conceit about the roasted youngsters' jellied eyes was to me disgusting. It was not worthy of the gentle Elia. He would not have been guilty of it had he ever stood, as I have done many a day for half-an-hour at a time, watching the engaging gambols of a young litter, seen best when fresh straw had been thrown them. There is no more charming picture of animal infancy. Here a roguish eye appears, there a moist shining disc of nose working anticipatively in the hope of provender that your coming has aroused. One sportive little chap seizes a long straw in his mouth and frisks off with it, champing his jaws in pretended relish, another shakes his head till his neck smacks with the long, silken ears, then parades round rakish, with one ear turned inside out. This moment they are all fun and gambol, one jumping over another, or two or three butting a comrade down and nosing him playfully ; the next they form a group before the door, eyeing you with inquiring gravity, then in a sudden impulse scatter diverse through the straw again, squealing in affected panic. There was better matter and more akin to the mild spirit of Elia in such a sight than in the horrid spectacle of a roasted innocent. He might have given us a chapter on tails, and shown us with infinite adornment of fancy how that little embellishment of one end of a pig can modify the character of the other end of him ; how the accident of a straight tail can throw a subtle suggestion of melancholy over a snub and cheerful countenance, or a curly tail bestow a certain archness on a long, serious snout.

To an Irish boy Lamb's transports over the flavour of sucking pigs seemed unnatural and ghoulish. We Irish have a repugnance to immature meats. We do not reckon sucking-pig among our dishes. I would as soon think of eating a baby.

But Charles was punished for his repulsive preference. He never knew pig at its best. He does not seem to have known the incomparable lusciousness (he would have called it sapor) of stuffed pork fillets. From his remark about " the rank bacon " he can have enjoyed no breakfast dallyings with mild-cured Irish such as my Cousin Joseph— esteemed a connoisseur—used to deal out to me some morning after I had been storm-stayed at his house, accompanying the generous helping with his time-honoured joke that " *there* was something better than Shakespeare."

Yet it was bacon that prevented my ever having a pig for my friend. The butcher's knife hung suspended over the most captivating youngster of our rearing. I could not bear to embark on a friendship of which the end must inevitably be tragedy. I knew too well the warnings of doom, the straw scattered in the yard, the cauldron of boiling water, the beam in winter laid along the rafters of the barn, in summer resting on two branches of the great ash tree—the sledge hammer and cord. Already I saw the carcasses hideously suspended. It was no mere porcine tragedy that my imagination bodied forth. Romance and history swelled the scene. Perhaps the Great Marquis had met his pitiful fate ; or I was in the Middle Ages, and Villon and his associates hung pendent from the gallows.

But had I been transported back to a sterner century, I could never have made one of the jeering crowd at a gallows' foot. When our dog Keeper's furious baying told me that Pat D——, the pig-sticker, was at hand, I fled to my bedroom and remained there with muffled ears till the execution was over in all its grisly details. I only once emerged from my retreat before the carcasses were cleaned and hung up ; it was because I wished to know exactly what happened to Vich Ian Vohr and Evan Maccombich after they drove off from Waverley on the hurdle ; and I wish I hadn't done it. Ever afterward Pat D—— was to me " a horrid fellow as beseemed his trade." He perceived my distaste for him ; and being a kindly man, as I know now, and fond of children, used to propitiate me with bladders. But a pig's bladder makes a lopsided football, with no accuracy of flight. I had little pleasure in Pat's gifts, and wasn't softened towards him.

My emotions of horror were transient. Before nightfall I was looking forward eagerly to next morning's drive to the pork-market; that is, if I had obtained permission to accompany old Tom Brogan, who as a steady, faithful retainer of thirty years' standing and more was generally trusted to sell our pork. The best market was nine miles away. To arrive in time it was necessary in winter that the cart should leave our house about five o'clock. It was the only early rising that was ever pleasant to me. But everything connected with it was full of novelty and charm. On such a morning a little boy might wash in the most perfunctory fashion unreproved. Then there was the delight of having breakfast in the kitchen with Tom Brogan, and mopping up my bacon-gravy with crusts, and cooling my tea in the saucer, just as he did. For our maid-servants were always too sleepy to reprove my breaches of table manners, and my aunt, conscious of the undress beneath her shawl, issued her instructions to Tom in a series of hoverings round the kitchen door, but never ventured in. I had my tea strong those mornings, and ate twice as much breakfast as usual, and in half my usual time, the latter part of the meal degenerating into mere cramming as my uncle's muffled roars from upstairs became more insistent. When I had gulped down the last possible mouthful of tea—the hottest one—I was pounced upon by our maid and wrapped in such superfluity of mufflers that it became necessary to shake the breath half out of my body before my overcoat would button. Then I mounted the box seat

of the stage-coach—for I was generally Tom Brown
going to Rugby on such occasions—and off we
went.

I shall never forget those early morning drives,
though I cannot recall the details of any one of
them. They are all compounded into a single
experience. There is the sensation of darkness and
intense cold. The lantern shadows wheel slowly on
the trees as our yard boy lights us down the avenue.
The lantern hangs in the air without human agency
as I look behind me and call good-bye. The ice
crashes under our wheels; our horse snorts and
clatters as he mounts the hill, fearful of the frozen
road. We emerge from the trees, and there a pale
moon is hanging strangely in the west. Presently
we settle down to a steady jog. A phantasmagoria
of tree and hedge shapes passes sleepily before my
eyes. Across the fields sounds the rattle of another
cart, bound as I know, on a like errand with ourselves. Another and another is heard as we draw
near the four roads. The countryside is filled with
the soothing murmur of innumerable carts, all
going to D—— pork-market. I am lying on the
straw and Tom Brogan is covering me with a rug.
I peer drowsily over the edge of the cart; we are
one of a long procession of carts. Trees and houses
are taking on colour; here and there a lighted
window gleams warmly in the pallid dawn. I close
my eyes; and next moment I am staggering on
numbed feet in the pork-market of D——, and Tom

Brogan is peering into my face and asking me if I am sure I am awake.

Row upon row of carts fill up the market square. I scamper in and out, and am disconcerted to find that our pigs are not the wonders of the pork world I thought them. I hurry back to warn Tom. He is surrounded by several sharp-faced men with pencils and note-books. They are pork-buyers, city men ; the name of a great bacon-curing firm in Belfast is mentioned. I feel myself a country boy, and am abashed before them, and forbear to warn Tom. But I fume with anxiety when he refuses the offered price, and know in my heart he is making a mistake, and that we shall return home ignominious with our pigs unsold. I cannot bear the strain, but go off again among the carts, and am diverted from my anxiety by observing, rather to my disgust, sundry other boys from our school enjoying a holiday on pork-market day. I return to our cart. The pigs are sold. I am delighted with our success ; but feel that Tom took great risks, and wonder at his nerve.

Then Tom and I go to what he calls an eating-house, and I have steak and onions, and strong tea again, and fresh bread in thicker slices than I had ever seen before, and do not die of it all as I should now, but hurry off to buy sweets with the sixpence that Tom has been authorized to give me, and to watch the roulette table, and the man with three thimbles and a pea. I perceive that this last is a simple fellow, and am sorry I have spent my sixpence, and suggest a loan from Tom ; but he tells me such men have the Black Art, and that I would only lose my money ; so I press him no more, but avoid evil, and pass on to the Aunt Sally.

But my early rising begins to tell on me. My appetite for pleasure is dulled sooner than usual. I begin to have a curious sensation that all the movement around me is happening in a dream. Besides, I am anxious to get home again, to tell everybody how well Tom and I have sped in our marketing. So when the cart is ready I climb in willingly enough. I feel a little sad on the homeward journey. It is probably the steak and onions ; but I do not know that, and think I am sorry about the dead pigs. When I have had my supper, I go to look at the empty piggery, and feel really sorry when I remember its departed occupants, their tumultuous rush to the gate when they heard my footsteps, their cheerful upraised snouts and interrogative gruntings, their luxurious submission to my scratching of their backs with the handle of the yard shovel. These were the nearest approaches to friendship I ever made with our pigs. On the evening of pork-market days I was always sorry I had gone so far.

HARVEST

IN the crafts of ploughing and sowing and reaping
my childish days were nearer to the times of Homer
and the Old Testament than to the present. A hind
of Ithaca might have beheld with small wonder the
swing-plough of my boyhod, or Ruth have gleaned
after a scythe without amazement. But the coming
tiller of the soil will have no portion in the long
tradition of man's dealings with his mother earth.
The curse of Adam will have been lifted from him.
He will no longer earn his bread by the sweat of
his brow. The sons of Adam will soon delve no
more, just as the daughters of Eve have long ceased
to spin. Doubtless the profit will be great ; but
there will be losses. The little boy of to-morrow will
eat fine bread and plentiful, but he will never see
Tom Brogan go forth, with one of my aunt's sheets
slung round his neck, to illustrate the parable of the
Sower as neither woodcut nor etching could do.
As I watched a sowing-machine to-day, my mind
travelled far from these mechanical times. I saw
old Tom in a field of County Down, and marked his
measured pace and rhythmical swinging arm as he
sowed the good seed. It was always Tom who
sowed the good seed in our yearly re-enactment of

the parable. The thistles and the charlock I blamed on squint-eyed Peter Tumelty, and likened him to the Adversary.

The interregnum between seed-time and harvest has furnished me with few memories of the farm. My summer recollections are filled with fishing, and cricket and bathing, and picnics, and the exotic pleasures of the seaside. I was less of a country boy in summer, strangely enough. But with harvest time the spell of the country fell on me again. My mind is stored with pictures of that sweetest of all seasons. They come to me in capricious glimpses ; the bright flame of corn-poppies ; purple tints of field-scabious ; the white haze in the zenith, here and there elbow-worn to blue ; the barred clouds, strangely moveless ; the mellow radiance of the sunshine ; the glistening gossamers ; brown-grey islands of hay-cocks in the green after-grass ; stiff stooks of wheat, and gracious oat-stooks, drawn in long ranks across the stubble. The berries of the honeysuckle are red in the hedge ; the propeller-blades of the sycamore fruit are reddening ; one side of the haws has turned reddish-brown. The blackberry clusters are dull as yet ; but here and there one hangs shining and luscious among the dark green leaves. The life of the year is waning ; yet its very decay reveals that it has not been lived in vain ; as if a righteous man should die and leave his good works visibly behind him on the tomb.

I have many another treasure of memory in my

harvest storehouse, albeit a little disorderly arranged. The Common is ripe, and must be " opened " before the reaping-machine can be set to work. I listen to the steady swish of Tom Brogan's scythe as he moves along the sward, remorseless as Time, that if Tom but knew it has nearly come to the end of one Tom Brogan's swathe of life. The old man pauses and wipes the wet grass from his scythe-blade. I hear his whetstone ringing cheerily on the steel. Now the reaper is lumbering and rattling along. Our bay mare Betty snatches a stolen mouthful of oats, then throws her head high to the driver's admonishing pluck of the rein. William Brown, perched aloft in his jolting seat, shepherds the severed corn-stalks with oar-like movements of his rake, and leans sideways to dismiss each sheaf with caressing pressure. The following women lift the sheaves knee-high, tie them in one deft movement, then toss them aside and explore their horny hands for thistle spines till the reaping machine comes round again.

My part in all this activity was that of a busy idleness. I scampered about, " like a dog at a fair," in old Tom's phrase, now officious with oil-can or spanner, now acting as assistant surgeon when a fragment of thistle proved unusually refractory, now fetching water from the spring-well to refresh the thirsty workers. Sometimes I had a short spasm of industry, and made half-a-dozen straps to bind sheaves. The straps were made of two handfuls

of corn-straw united by a cunning twist. But my
twist lacked cunning, or perhaps it was vigour that
was wanting. I knew that the straps of my making
would never lie till I had the sheaf safely placed
thereon. They kept untwisting all the time I was
gathering up my sheaves, and though I hoped for
the best, would never withstand the final tug before
tying, but always gave way and scattered the oats
or wheat dishevelled on the sward. I remember
that in my earliest harvest I had an impulse of
frugality, and fell to gleaning, or " gathering heads,"
as we called it in County Down. But I found it
back-breaking work, and was very glad when old
Jenny Mason, on whose perquisite I was infringing,
pointed out to me what a serious injustice I was
doing to herself and her pig.

Now and then, when money was plentiful among
our hands, I would be commissioned to purvey
bottled stout from Barney D——'s public-house.
I esteemed such days lucky ; for apart from my
wage of lemonade (that nostril-tickling delight of
youth), there was much scouting to be done on the
return journey lest I should be detected by my uncle,
recondite hiding-places to be devised, and mysterious
indications given. Every afternoon I had a task of
legitimate usefulness, that I didn't enjoy nearly so
much, in helping to bring out the canful of tea and
basket of buttered farls of bread for the afternoon
tea-meal, then first appearing in the countryside,
portent of luxury and declining pith. But I cracked

my little cheeks over farls two inches deep, and drank my tea out of a tin, and spread the lumps in my butter with my thumb, the same as Tom Brogan, and was not without my reward. For the most part, however, I was content with sloth. Snug in my bower of sheaves I husked oats or wheat between my palms, and was a hermit eating pulse ; or dissected scarlet berries of the wild-rose, and munched the sweet rind, and longed to test whether one of the hairy seeds would really choke me if I ate, but never found courage for the experiment ; or rolled the cobwebby film on the coltsfoot leaf into fragile thread, and rejoiced in the young fresh green beneath. Last joy of reaping time, it was my privilege to cut the ultimate wisp of grain, that it might be woven into the " churn " to hang from our kitchen ceiling till next harvest. Then I distributed the ritual half-crowns and whisky for which—alas for old custom—the former " churn-supper " had been commuted, and felt myself quite the young squire, but never could see why I, who got no whisky, should be fobbed off with sixpence.

After the reaping time came Harvest Home with its own peculiar joys. First of all there was the " whummling " of the stooks that the wind might blow through the sheaves as they lay prone. To a little boy with a rake, and some miscellaneous reading, and any imagination at all, an orgy of chivalry lay open. Foes stood before him in battalions, and could be overwhelmed in half-dozens at a time. But though the mark was easy, triumph was by no means so certain as you might suppose. Given a cluster of stout sheaves, and a rake-handle in the fervour of combat directed incautiously towards a small solar plexus, and I have known victory to shine on the wrong side of the hedge.

Better things came with the " drawing-in." A farm-cart furnished with the iron frame on which the load was built made no bad chariot. On a straight course, and with Betty in the shafts, I would have challenged any Roman that ever careered round a Stadium ; though perhaps a really ex-perienced Roman would have taken the turning into the Haw-Hill with more judgment, and avoided bringing the gate-post with him. After that fatal day I drove afield no more. I was little disconcerted. It was but a change of pleasures. William Brown became Cebriones to my Hector. Secure in such a driver I hurled my vengeful spear and slew whole stooks of Greeks.

I had a further portion in the drawing-in when the laden cart was " up-ended " in the haggard and poured a tumbling cascade of plenty along the ground. I yielded to no one in the nice calculation of where a boy might stand so that the torrent of sheaves would foam just to his feet, though I don't mind admitting that in the learning stages I once or twice stood nearer the cart than the back of my head would have chosen. When stack-building

began I always had business elsewhere, after the
first years of vanity.   I would counsel all little boys
to do the same.   For the building of stacks has not
yet become a matter of machinery ; and grown-ups
have a thoughtless habit of summoning little boys
to tread down the sheaves as they are laid.   A very
hot and wearisome business that, and fills the boots
with lead.   The subsequent glide down the long
ladder is by no means worth the price.

Perhaps if you had been standing in our haggard
later on, when the stack was being taken down, you
would have said I enjoyed that process most of all.
And it cannot be denied that for bustle and activity
it ranks high among farming operations.   From the
moment when Tom Brogan threw the body of
Admiral Coligny off the top of the stack to the
ravening adherents of the House of Guise below,
my excitement rose in a climax till he reached the
last few tiers of sheaves, where the rats and mice
ate their Belshazzar's feast.   With the dropping of
the first mouse or rat to the ground uproar began.
Women cast down their pitchforks and fled shrieking ; men ran diverse with laughter and shouts,
beating the ground furiously, half time in vain.
Terriers yelped and ran and pounced and slew, and
turned again to slaying.   Jock the sheep dog barked
louder still ; but found one mouse an afternoon's
employment, and let it escape in the end.   If there
was a pig abroad in the farmstead, and there
generally was, he somehow found himself in the

middle of the fuss. The very hens and ducks had their share in the fun. The ducks, wise as their wont, lurked underneath the framework of the stack, and guzzled mice to repletion ; the hens fluttered and squawked out of the rat-killers' way and into it again, reaping little advantage. Here and there among the stacks a hen wandered in apparent unconcern with a mouse's tail hanging from her mouth ; but her apoplectic and misgiving eye suggested regret for the easier paths of vege-tarianism. In the middle of all the turmoil you might have seen a little boy running about, armed with a big stick, and clamouring for the blood of rats. But if you had been inside that little boy, as I was, you would have known that the one thing he was anxious to avoid was an encounter with a rat ; and that he was even pacifically disposed towards mice, and very much relieved when the massacre of both sorts had been accomplished, and he might lay aside his stick and boast of the slain.

THE CHRISTMAS RHYMERS

THERE is a small white scar just on the crown of my head, now almost effaced by time. I wish it were not quite so faint. I received the wound many Christmases ago at the hands of no less a personage than Saint George. If you have met him the night he did the deed you would not have recognized him. He would appear to you in the shape of a sturdily-built youth of about fourteen. His body would be shrouded in a ragged white shirt, clearly the cast-off of an older and larger man, and girt about the waist with a rope of straw. The lower portion of his legs would be bound with straw-rope also. On his head instead of a halo there would be a top hat many sizes too large, tilted back to prevent his being completely engulfed, and wreathed with parti-coloured ribbon. Your natural curiosity to behold the countenance of a saint would be frustrated by a pasteboard vizard of horrific lineaments. On the whole you would have been in doubt whether you were looking at a saint at all, and if you had known as much about him as I did you would have been quite certain about it.

But do not suspect me of bearing malice. Saint George and I have shaken hands long ago, and are friends of, alas! how many years' standing. When we meet we forget the war and talk long of old times and pleasant memories. Not the least pleasant were the nights when he and I went Christmas-rhyming together, enacting the fragments, however debased, of a drama in which the original cast may have been Druids, and helping to keep alive a little longer the embers of an expiring tradition.

The members of our little company come back to me one by one. Some are alive, though changed ; and others being dead are changeless. Little Tom Torrens still lives, and has married a wife twice as big as himself, and begotten sons and daughters at least half-a-score. It was for this quality of hardiness, even then apparent in him, that we chose him as our prologue, who must first spring from the sheltering darkness into the lighted kitchen where we found our stage, and foreshadow our mystery. His voice was, like himself, small ; but it was shrill and clear enough, and he made a brave prologue :

Room, room, brave and gallant boys, come give us room
    to rhyme,
We come to show activity about these Christmas times,
Active youth and active age, the like was never acted on
    the stage,
And if you don't believe what I say enter in St. George
    and he'll clear the way.

It was only last week that I heard young Tom—the latest of Old Tom's family except the twins—declaim the lines to an admiring kitchen-full of his relatives. He did it with a good deal of spirit and vigour, too ; and his voice—it came to him from his mother's side of the house—is deeper than old Tom's was at his age ; but though I didn't care to say so, I thought he wasn't a patch on what his father used to be.

I wil not tell you what Saint George's name was in private life. Saint George has made money and bought land, and cuts some figure in the country. He is an elder of his Kirk these twenty years, and though he likes to talk with me in private about his Christmas Rhyming days, and some other small follies of his youth, I don't think he would like his family to know about them.

Robbie McKillop was our Oliver Cromwell. Peace be with him—he is dust these many years ; but he was weak in the part. My Cousin Barbara, despite her sex, was worth a dozen of him ; but happening to catch sight of herself one night in an unexpected looking-glass was so alarmed by her own false-face with its portentous nose that she fell into hysterics, and threw up the part just as she was letter-perfect ; so we had to fall back upon Robbie.

Our " Doctor " was one Dick Semple, now also with the shades. His presence caused some scandal among the parents of our troupe ; for his birth was esteemed humbler than became the company ; but the demands of art prevailed. The " Doctor " was our comic part, and Dick was inimitable in it.

Chubby little Mary Grant, as befitted the future

mistress of a gaunt three-storied farmhouse, plied
the broom of Little Devil Doit as lustily as could be
desired ; but I marvel now at our sense of the fitness
of things when we cast Winnie B—— for Beelzebub.
Surely a gentler spirit was never wronged by such a
part, or a milder, sweeter countenance obscured by
pasteboard wickedness.   But she was tall and slim
of shape, and cut a gallant figure in a red silk blouse,
and a pair of her mother's long stockings, and
scarlet trunks, with her skirts stuffed inside in the
cause of propriety.   If the real Prince of Darkness
was abroad any of those murky nights, and we
sometimes suspected it, he must have gnashed his
teeth to see purity and innocence go by in his image.
It was for Winnie's sweet sake I suffered by Saint
George's sword.   The fleeting touch of two cold lips
on mine has left a more abiding wound than that it
recompensed.

For weeks before Christmas my Cousin Joseph's
corn-loft was the scene of much sewing and snipping,
and desperate contrivances of ribbons and patches
not always lawfully acquired.   No fragment of
bright material was secure to our elders in the month
of December.   My aunt long deplored a remnant
of green satin she lost one winter, and never knew
it went to grace Saint Patrick's helm.   Our ill-gotten
finery never stayed with us.   However glorious we
went forth any Christmas, the following one found
us once more naked and predatory.   For masks we
sponged on my Cousin Joseph, and never in vain.

Each Christmas he unbuttoned his pockets he swore it was for the last time ; but we knew Cousin Joseph better than that.

It was always a very compact little band that travelled the roads on performing nights. In our pretended characters we felt ourselves more obnoxious than usual to the Powers of Darkness. It was safe enough to presume on the benevolence of Saint Patrick and Saint George towards our travesty of them ; but then we had Beelzebub and Devil Doit among us, and never felt sure how the originals might take it. And though we carried a lantern we seldom dared to display the light. For one thing it was necessary to approach our victims' houses unperceived. But in addition to that, the appearance of a grotesquely-painted mask thrown up suddenly against the darkness is trying to nerves already a little on the strain. Dick Semple once paused unknown to us, to tie his bootlace, and when our lantern was flashed on him as he came running after, we took to our heels and ran a quarter of a mile. Even grown-ups found our false faces too much for them. Many a farmhouse door was barred early on our account for weeks before Christmas, not without reason. It was said that John Dorrian's first-born came untimely into the world through his mother's looking up from her seat by the kitchen hearth to behold the door " with dreadful faces thronged." There is a mark on her offspring's cheek to this day that every old woman in the

country declares is the counterpart of Oliver Cromwell's nose. It is true that her doctor derided any
connection between the two happenings; and I
incline to believe him; but it cannot be denied that
our irruptions sometimes were the cause of more
alarm than mirth. I myself saw Peter James Dolan
sit down in a crock of cream well ripe for churning,
at the entrance of prologue; and though Cousin
Joseph knew Peter James too well to believe he
sacrificed the balance of the cream, he indemnified
him for the irreparable ruin of his market-day
trousers. I had a good set-off against the liability,
having suffered damage in the same region through
the action of Peter James's agent, an Irish terrier;
for Peter James in his wrath had carried out an oft-
repeated threat to " put the dog on us "; but I was
too bashful to disclose it at the time, and let my
cousin pay.

It was a matter of some strategy to gain an
entrance to many houses. When after cautious
raising of a latch we found a door barred we fell back
on guile. Little Tom Torrens was our Sinon on
these occasions. Knocking boldly on the door he
tuned his piping voice to a pathetic key, and sobbed
out some concocted tale of disaster. He had tripped
over a stone and cut his knees on the road and
required first-aid; or had fallen in a drain on his
way home across the fields and needed drying; or
he had been going to Jervis's shop for a loaf, and had
dropped his sixpence, and could they let him have a

blink of light, for if the sixpence were lost he would be beaten when he went home. No Greek that ever entered the Wooden Horse was wilier than little Tom. The tragedy in his voice would have melted rocks, let alone the heart of a farmer's wife with boys of her own. All this time we stood in a bunch at his elbow, breathless, creeping closer and closer with each sign of relenting within, ready to thrust in our sticks the instant a line of light along the door-post showed that the citadel was breached. Then with a headlong rush the door was flung back, and we poured tumultuously into the kitchen, not seldom over the prostrate body of the sentinel; and faithless Tom, bounding into the middle of the kitchen, broke into "Room, room!" with all the shrillness of triumph. But having once gained an entrance we were never cast into outer darkness again until our play was played out. Perhaps no one was greatly deceived by our wiles.

In most farmhouses, indeed, we were received with pleasure. The floor was cleared of chairs to enlarge our stage. The grown-ups perched on tables to enjoy the show, with the elder boys and girls kneeling behind and peering over their shoulders; and sleepy children were brought rosy-faced and yawning from their beds, very often to return thither shrieking. In general, the mothers among our audience witnessed the show from "the room" door, half-strangled by the arms of a clutching youngster, with one or two of the less terrified

peering from the folds of her skirts, herself laughing
and soothing in alternate breaths, and patting the
affrighted one with comfortable hand. In such a
house we ate and drank plenteously, and put money
in our purse.

Yet strangely enough it is not our triumphs I
recall most clearly. Far more vividly I remember
the darkness, and the lashing rain, and the distant
soughing wind, and tossing branches against pale
rifts in the tattered clouds ; or on our rare hard
nights, the crackling rut-pools, and frosted hedges,
and glittering rimy fields. I remember our night-
alarms of moving sheep and belated cows, and the
terror of angry dogs ; and the Christmas Eve Devil
Doit fell into the mill-race, and the night we saw the
corpse-lights in the Quaggy bog. It was when I
wishéd to recall our old rhymes that I found great
gaps in my memory, and could not even remember
my old part of Saint Patrick. But I pieced them
together at last with fragments gathered here and
there, and had many a pleasant hour in the doing of
it, and fought my mimic battles over again, and made
new friends of some old friends, and threw off the
burden of years.

Perhaps the result was not worth my pains. I
have recovered no famous drama, long lost to the
world, no recondite specimen of folklore at which
the antiquary may rejoice and fall a-writing to learned
journals. The verses halt a little with their long
journey down the centuries, and have picked up

strange company by the way. But some little boy
or girl may like to sit for a space in an Ulster kitchen
of thirty years ago, and listen to the Christmas
Rhymers. Perhaps after a while they may find
some of their seniors at their elbow. Fling open the
door, then, Tommy Torrens, and declaim your
prologue. Come with me out of the shadows, my
little company, and we will speak our lines once
more.

You have learned what Saint George was like.
Imagine a husky bass rising now and then dis-
concertingly to treble :

Here comes I, Saint George, from England I have sprung,
One of these great and noble deeds a volume to begin.
I was seven long years in a close cave kept,
From there into a prison leapt,
From there bound to a rocky stone,
Where I gave many a sad and grievous moan.
I fought them all courageously,
And still I gained the victory.
Show me the man,
How dare he stand,
I'll cut him down with my courageous hand.

This is my cue to enter, armed, like Saint George,
with wooden sword and buckler.

Here comes I, Saint Patrick, with my shining arms so
    bright.
I am a famous champion by the day or by the night.
Who are you but Saint George—Saint Patrick's boy !
Who fed his horse on oats and hay,
And afterwards he ran away.

Saint George :

I say, by George, you lie, sir.

Saint Patrick :

Pull out your sword and try, sir.
I'll run my rapier through your body, and make you run
    away, sir.

Then what a clatter of wood on wood before
Saint George falls ! Our combat is not all feigning.
We fight for a fair lady, as saints have been known
to do before they put off their human nature. Saint
George strikes home—very much out of his part—
and drops at once, cunning rascal, to avoid reprisal,
and I, though burning for revenge, must pretend
ruth and call for succour :

A doctor, a doctor, ten pounds for a doctor !
Is there not a doctor to be found
To cure this man of his deep and deadly wound ?

And now behold Dick Semple, our comedian and
star, with bearded mask, and monstrous phial.
But you do not know our Dispensary doctor's
shambling walk and thin cracked voice, and so will
not give Dick credit for his artistry.

Yes, here comes I, old Doctor Scott,
The best old doctor of the lot.
If this man's life I mean to save,
Forty guineas I must have.

Saint Patrick :

What can you cure, Doctor ?

Doctor :

I can cure the plague within the plague, the palsy or the
  gout.

Saint Patrick :

What's your medicine, doctor ?

Doctor :

The rue, the rue,
Brock's dew,
Hog's lar',
Pitch and tar,

The sap of the poker, the juice of the tongs,
Three turkey-cock's eggs nine yards long.
Put these in a hen's bladder,
And stir up with a cat's feather,—
And if Jack's a living man he'll get up and sing.

Saint George (rises and sings) :

Wonderful, wonderful, the like was never seen,
For a stout young fellow about the age of nineteen.
I've run with the buck, fought with the bear,
And rode with the devil on his old grey mare.
And if you don't believe what I say
Enter in Oliver Cromwell and he'll clear the way.

The announcement is not needed ; his nose
bespeaks him. If we are near the end of our Season
it is a little battered about the tip. One does not
easily safeguard such a nose on dark nights.

Here comes I, Oliver Cromwell, as you may suppose,
I've conquered many nations with my long copper nose,
I've made the French to tremble and the Spaniard to
  quake,

And I've fought the bloody Dutchman till I made his
    heart ache.
And if you don't believe what I say
Enter in Beelzebub and he'll clear the way.

Steal softly in, little Winnie, and speak your lines
unabashed.   No one but I can see the sweet pale face
behind your flaming vizard.   Deal tenderly with the
devil as you were wont, and still call him Beelthebub.
We will weep rather than laugh to hear your lisping
now.   And you, children, listen intently, for Beelzebub is nervous, and will be very breathless before
he has finished his lines, and his voice will trail away
to a whisper.

> Here comes I, Beelzebub,
> Over my shoulder I carry my club,
> And in my hand a dripping pan,
> I think myself a jolly old man.
> And if you don't believe what I say
> Enter in Devil Doit and he'll clear the way.

Be patient ; our play is nearly ended.   But let
the head of the family get ready his penny when
Devil Doit rattles the money-box.   The floor is
earthen, and Devil Doit is very handy with his
broom.   He gives you fair warning :

Here comes I, wee Devil Doit,
If you don't give me money I'll sweep you all out.
Money I want and money I crave,
If you don't give me money I'll sweep you all to your
    grave.

Come away from the dust and the laughter. The curtain has fallen, and will not rise again. There is no money for little Devil Doit nowadays. His broom has become old-fashioned, and would be out of place in a city parlour. Play your own games, children. We of another generation will look on awhile and be merry with you. You must not mind if some of us presently steal away thirty years or so, and spend our Christmas in the country. We shall not be quite so merry there ; but there will be a smile on our lips, and our hearts will be very tender.

FIRES

I was fond of low company as a child. I loved
the society of ploughmen, and cattle dealers, and
"tradesmen," as we call carpenters and masons
and such-like in the North of Ireland ; and on occasion was even not above consorting with tinkers.
But greatest of all pleasures was to slip out of a
winter's night to some labourer's or small farmer's
cottage and take part in a kailyie. We are more
learned now, and know the word for Irish and spell
it *c.e.l.e.i.d.h* ; but it meant just the same then,
a gathering of neighbours in friendly chat round
a hearthside.

Our servant-maids were scandalized by my want
of proper pride. Many a time they threatened to
" tell on me," and now and then carried out their
threat. But my aunt, although she had plenty of
pride, had a good deal of common-sense as well,
and winked at my unconventionality. It would do
the child no harm, I have overheard her say, to see
a little of all sorts.

I think she was right, too, and that it did not do
me any harm. If I saw and heard much that was
coarse and unseemly, I saw and heard much, too,

that was simple and pure and uplifting. If I learned a little evil, I learned a great deal more good. The evil fell away from me as I grew in knowledge ; but the good remains with me to this day. There was many a worse school for a little boy than an Ulster hearthside thirty years ago. And I count it something that I can still sit down in a cottier dwelling and talk to a labourer and his family in their own homely speech, and enter into their humble joys and sorrows with sympathy and understanding. In those days it did not enter my head that I belonged to a different race of beings. I am not sure that I have learned the lesson yet.

The humbler folk among whom I visited were much more ready to recognize a difference between them and me. Although I was received among them on familiar terms, some little acknowledgment of my higher standing was always insisted on. If among the family circle and its intimates I was always addressed by my Christian name, should a stranger be present it was scrupulously prefixed by the respectful " Master." One of " the room " chairs was always set out for me to take my place by the hearth. It was a poor household indeed that could not afford me the luxury of at least deal. At first I preferred to sit on one of the common chairs, the seats of which were composed of straw ropes wound on a wooden framework. But I found that the newest was always offered me, and the asperities of such a seat, with its projecting ends of corn stalks, require a certain amount of discipline by corduroy before they cease to trouble the wearer of cloth.

Perched on my seat of honour I have in my time mottled my boyish shins at many kinds of flame. The dullest to me was a coal fire, such as a middling farmer's house would offer. We had coal fires at home. Then to enjoy a coal fire to the full one should be alone. In its early stages, with a good gassy coal, it is true that as many can be happy round it as can provide themselves with pokers. I have even known an expert, skilled in the due moment to puncture the swelling shiny coal bubble, monopolize a solitary poker to the common satisfaction ; and have had ambitions in that direction myself. But when smoke has dwindled, and the coals are glowing and falling lower in the grate, more than one fire-gazer is a crowd. The castle that I see so plainly is perhaps a craggy summit to another pair of eyes, or the lion's head a horse. Two souls must surely be in perfect harmony to read the fiery architecture alike. When I hear of such a thing I am tempted to suspect that there is more than fire-gazing between them.

I know it was so with myself as a boy of eleven and little Lucy D——, the only daughter in one of my coal-fire houses. She was a timid little creature with pretty pinched features and flaxen hair that would not curl for all her mother could do, born to worship aggressive small boys and to bend the neck gladly before a tyrannical husband, and fade beneath the strain of bringing up his rowdy family.

K

I do not think I was an aggressive small boy ; but I was her social superior by some fifty acres, and she looked up to me, and gave me her love.

I used to visit early at that house, before the regular kailyie began.   Side by side we pored over the grate, and I drank in the sweetness of her submissiveness to my interpretation of the fiery oracles.   When I remember Lucy's elf-like little face, it is always framed in an aureole of flame-lit hair.   But presently a serpent entered into my Eden, a sturdy youth some twelve months my senior ; and I knew the first pangs of jealousy when Lucy began to reject my romantic visions for his prosaic imaginings. I contended with him for some time in a losing struggle, till at last one evening he invited me out to fight, over a unicorn that he maintained was a donkey.   I still think it was a unicorn, and with Lucy's support would have had faith even to single combat ; but she sided with my rival ; and I quitted the field with an obvious retort the recollection of which comforted me a little in my humiliation.   I had to fight him next day, after all, for calling him a donkey, and in the stress of battle it came into my mind that I might just as well have been fighting for my unicorn and Lucy's love.   But he worsted me rather badly, and I see now that it didn't matter.

In my humbler visiting circle there were few coal fires.   A man with a wage amounting at the best to twelve shillings a week can do little to swell the royalties of Coal Kings.   But there are many other

means of raising a blaze ; and any of them is more
alluring than coal. I have often listened to the
crackling of thorns under a pot, and relish the
phrase more than one who has heard it only with his
mind's ear. Nevertheless, thorns are a disap-
pointing fuel, showy, but of little efficacy, and
associated in the farmer's mind, not without reason,
with open gaps and straying cattle. I liked their
cheerful crackle. The aftermath of glowing twigs
will etch a picture with a freedom of line unknown
to coal. But I was not always ignorant of the source
of supply, and I had some mental struggles between
the honour of a guest and the duty of a nephew.

The steady radiance of well-lighted turf places
it high in the ranks of poor man's fuel. For myself
I never took to it. Like the tang of goat's milk, the
smell of turf has always remained an exotic flavour
to my senses. My aunt disliked it for a different
reason. She esteemed it a Roman Catholic fuel, and
not quite fit burning for the dominant creed. There,
too, a masterful uncle need be no Sherlock Holmes
to divine from the aroma of a small boy's clothes
that he has not been visiting in the highest circles
the night before; and my aunt's broad-mindedness
in the matter of companionship was not shared by
her husband, except about his own associates.
For these causes, unless the company promised
something above the ordinary, I generally avoided
turf-burning cottages.

Wood was my favourite kailyie fire. Even green

branches have their merits, of bubbling sap and hissing moisture, soft under-song to the dancing kettle lid. And what can make a cleaner or more cheerful fire than a pile of split logs, ash for choice ? I cannot see a noble tree felled now without a pang as for a life untimely taken. But, then, the blazing logs awakened no misgivings in my mind, too intent on my self-imposed task of stoker to remember that some glory of the woodlands was being threatened by my zeal. And as the night drew on and the bright pile shuddered into ashes, how sweet to watch glow and shadow chase each other over the incandescent charcoal with every eddying draught, or project the unburned ends with wary toe and awaken the dying flame.

There was a pleasant flavour of the illicit about a log fire also. Trees were the property of the landlord, and might not be felled without his consent. But here conscience slumbered. I was a farmer's nephew, and my withers were unwrung. Few country consciences were more tender in such a matter. The common bond of advantage stilled both labourer's and farmer's tongue ; and many a tall tree fell unmarked of its lawful lord.

With a fire of " shoughs " one came in contact with poverty. Shoughs are the fragments of stalk beaten from flax fibre in the process of scutching. Small ends and wisps of the fibre are mingled with the shoughs. The whole furnishes the most evanescent of fires, with much blaze but little heat. A torrent of sparks pours up the chimney as it consumes, and this firework display can be augmented by tapping the mass with a poker, as I have been thoughtless enough to do many a time, and waste more rapidly my hostess's scanty store. I say my hostess's, for I visited in only one shough-burning cottage. Poor old Mary Kinner, I can see her now, squatted on the earthen floor of her one-roomed dwelling, knees close to chin, mumbling with toothless gums on the short-stemmed clay pipe, her only luxury, too often empty. She dwelt alone, the solitary survivor of her generation, so far sunk in years that, without dying, she might be said to have outlived life.

Mary was come of decent people, as the saying goes in the North ; and folk remembered this. Her pittance of parish relief was eked out by unasked charity. Without abounding, she lived a little on this side of want. Old as she was, the instinct of hospitality still remained with her. Her pocket was a widow's cruse, never empty of some fragment of " sweetie " to please a little boy.

She liked to have me come to her cottage. I had little to say ; for I was overawed by her antiquity ; but the desire of speech had departed from her. Human companionship was all she needed ; and there is something soothing to old age in the presence of a child.

I was always glad to visit Mary. I loved the shough fire, the quick-leaping flame as I cast on each handful, the pouring sparks, the restless afterglow. Not even Mary herself was more pleased when the tin "tea-drawer" hissed into steam, or rejoiced more when the twisted paper screw of mingled tea and sugar which she drew from her bosom was fat and promised rich liquor. When, as not seldom, it was meagre, and old Mary's face and her anxious stirring and reluctant pouring out presaged mere "water bewitched," my little heart ached as hers had long lost power to do, and I knew that our hapless servant girl would shortly be in for a wigging over a tea caddy uncannily depleted. Even now I cannot regret those charitable thefts. If they seared my conscience a little they kept my heart tender. And with it all I am quite sure our maids drank too much tea.

When Mary lighted her after-tea pipe I laid down the poker. She was the first woman I had ever seen smoke a pipe, and the performance had a strange fascination for me. Quiet fell on my restless limbs and spirit as I watched. I have sat for half a winter's evening gazing across the hearth at the old, age-weary face, as it brightened with each "draw" and darkened with each puff of smoke, the silence never broken except by Mary's muttered self-communings. We must have made a strange picture sitting by the dim hearth, without speech or movement, in some mysterious accord of childhood and old age.

Those quiet hours made a deeper impression on me than any other experience of my childhood.

Pity and sorrow awoke in me then. It was then that the first questionings on life and death stirred my soul. But my sorrow was for others, in whose sad lot I had no portion. I saw that old Mary must die, but was not conscious of my own mortality. It is otherwise with me now. Not long ago, rambling about my early haunts, I entered the roofless cottage that had been Mary's, and sat by the cold hearth. When I last sat there life stretched long before me. Infinite space divided me from the calamity of old age. Surely it was only yesterday; but now her remembered face brings with it the poignant knowledge that I, too, am growing old, and must go hence, and that the longest life is, after all, but a fire of shoughs.

THE OLD WOMAN

IT was a bitter evening in March—I mind it as well as yesterday, though I was only a boy of eleven at the time—when I met the little band of gipsies as I was coming home from my uncle's out-farm.

When I saw them I slipped in behind the pillar of a gate till they should pass; for the gipsies had a bad name in our part of the country, some saying they were kidnappers, and others that they had the Black Art; and it was falling dark at the time, and I was afraid.

I made sure the last of them was gone before I stepped out again, but just round the bend of the road I came on the old woman struggling along against the wind. Very tall she was, and gaunt-looking, and had on her an old black cloak with a hood, such as I've heard my aunt say they wore when she was a young girl.

I didn't mind the old woman very much, seeing she was by herself; and it was on my tongue to bid her good-night; but I thought better of it, and didn't say a word to her, nor she to me. But she looked at me for a moment, very keen and searching, and it seemed to me that her eyes under the hood were glowing like coals of fire.

As I went on up the road I couldn't get her out of my head, nor the look she gave me. I was afraid and yet I wasn't afraid; and all the time I felt as if there was something drawing me to her. Before I knew what I was doing I ran back and pulled her by the cloak, and asked her would she like to lie for the night in my uncle's barn.

She bade " God bless me," and said she would be very glad and grateful. And I took her back, and opened the barn door, and shook some straw down in the corner for her to sleep on, and found her an old horse-cover to put over her.

My heart was warmed with what I had done for the old woman, and I didn't stop at that, but went along to a cottier house and got her a mug of tea and some fresh soda bread. And she ate her supper by what light there was at the door of the barn, and thanked and blessed me again, and went in and lay down on the straw.

All the way home I was in two minds whether to tell my uncle what I had done; for he was a hard man, and I doubted he would blame me. But my conscience wouldn't let me keep it to myself, and I told him. He was furiously angry, as I expected, and cursed me for a sentimental young fool, that his barn would be burned down, and ordered me to go back at once and put the old woman out.

I pleaded with him for a long time, but he wouldn't listen; so I went back, very slowly and unwillingly, and when I opened the door of the barn and went in, sure enough, as my uncle had said, the old woman was smoking as she lay among the straw ; and worse than all, and what would have driven my uncle clean mad if he had seen it, she had lit a candle and propped it up between two bricks.

I was ready enough to turn her out when I saw that ; but just as I was about to speak she looked up at me, and at the look of her the words failed in my mouth ; for she was like nothing earthly lying there among the straw, with the long grey hair falling about her face and her eyes burning in the sockets like it might be in a dead skull.

I stood there, shifting from one foot to the other, and gazing at her, and all I could find to say after a while was that I hoped she was warm and comfortable.

" I am warm and comfortable this night," she said, " and it's thanks to you that I am that same. But that's not what your uncle told you to say when he sent you to put me out into the black night and the wind."

I never answered a word, but the blood chilled in my veins ; for it came into my mind that she couldn't know all that and be canny.

" Go back to your uncle," she said at last, " and tell him that I'll not go out this night, but will lie here warm and well happed till the morning ; and in the morning I'll go my way in peace. And tell him that his barn will not be burned down, but will stand for many a year, and be filled with a blessing that was none of his earning. And he will say that he will come and put me out with his own hands; but he will not; for there is a power above the hard and cruel that strives with them sometimes for their own good."

And with the way she said that I looked at her again, and the fear of her left me; for I saw that she was nothing but a poor old woman.

But I was full of curiosity and wonder to know how she could tell what my uncle had said to me; and at the last I plucked up heart and asked her how she knew, and if I could learn as well as herself. Above all, I said, I wanted to have some skill of telling fortunes and knowing the future. And the old woman answered me, Yes, that she could tell fortunes: "For how," said she, "could you live for a hundred years under the stars, as I have done, without learning wisdom?"

"But come," said she, "give me your hand, and first of all I'll tell your fortune, and after that I'll show you the skill of it as I have it myself. For my days under the sun and the stars are numbered, and it is on me that I shouldn't leave this world and take with me any virtue that I have learned there."

So she told me my fortune, looking at my hand; both what had happened and what was going to happen.

"And now," said she "mark me, and I'll tell

you what you must do. First of all, when a man asks you to tell his fortune, you will take his hand in yours and look at the palm of it. And at the same time you will clear your mind of every thought, till there is nothing in all wide eternity but the palm of a hand and you gazing at it. And presently the power of your mind will draw virtue from the person whose hand you hold, and you will tell their past life as if it was a story and they telling it with their own lips.

"But you must remember," said the old woman, "to make your mind clear and blank; for if you cannot do that," said she, "you will never tell a good fortune."

"And what about the future?" I asked the old woman.

"For the future," said she, "you will use the good sense that God has given you, and the teaching of the wide world and the stars that folk call experience and wisdom. If it's a handsome slip of a young girl comes to you, what will she be looking but to get married, and what would you tell her but that she will? For people still wants to shape the future by the desires of their hearts; and if you tell them the desire of their hearts, what matter if it should never come true; for who wouldn't rather deserve a good fortune than gain one?

"And you needn't fear to be open-handed with your good-luck," said she. "Good news is better than true news. Besides, what comes true of the fortune you speyed will be remembered, and all the rest will be forgotten."

" And is that all you can tell of the future ? " said I.   For I was disappointed that I should hear no wonderful thing.

" It is all that any man or woman can tell," said she, " and it is not a little to them that has the seeing eye and the understanding mind.   For in the history of what is gone by is the prophecy of what is to come ; only them that looks must have the great gifts of God."

When she had said this the old woman was silent for a long time, and smoked her pipe.

" But for all that," says she to herself very loud and sudden, " the great mist that hides the future has been lifted for a few persons since the beginning of the world, and who knows but I am one of them "

A kind of fear came on me again when she said that ; and I bade good-night to her, though she didn't heed me, and slipped away quietly out by the door and off home.

When I got home I told my uncle what the old woman had said, and he did not go to put her out, but cursed her for an old witch, and said that if his barn was burned down he would take it out of my hide in the morning.

Next day I rose up early and ran to look at the barn.   My heart leaped in my body when I saw that it was safe.

And I sat down on the stone stile beside the barn, and thought about the fortune that had been speyed for me.   Long and long I thought about it, and many a time I have thought of it since.   And some of it came true of itself, and some of it I made come true because of what the old woman had told me.

TO MY FRIEND R. V. W.

Our feet no more shall chase the ball,
Nor in the dance delight,
Our sun of life has reached its moon,
And now turns toward the night.

What then? Its evening beams diffuse
A clearer, mellower ray.
And in the fields that knew its strength
We see our children play.

Gazing, another morn of life
To dear remembrance springs ;
And, faintly sweet, across the years
Another laughter rings.